You Will Learn to Love Me

You Will
Learn to
Love Me

Susan
Chace

 Random House New York

Copyright © 1994 by Swain Enterprises
All rights reserved under International and Pan-American Copyright Conventions. Published in the United States by Random House, Inc., New York.

Library of Congress Cataloging-in-Publication Data
Chace, Susan.
    You will learn to love me / Susan Chace.—1st ed.
      p. cm.
    ISBN 0-394-58384-1
    1. Marriage—Fiction.   I. Title.
  PS3553.H18Y68 1994
  813'.54—dc20   93-40839

Manufactured in the United States of America on acid-free paper
98765432
First Edition

To what is, with respect

Acknowledgments

I would like to thank the Yaddo Foundation; my agent, Phyllis Wender; and the staff at Random House, most especially my editor, David Rosenthal, and my copy editor, Virginia Avery.

And I am so grateful to: Tim Brandoff, Marcelle Clements, K. C. Cole, Susan Colgan, Vincent Crapanzano, Lynne Hennecke, Grace Knowlton, Jane Kramer, Susan Lee, Suzannah Lessard, Lilla Lyon, Virginia Mailman, Sara Moss, Djenane Nakhle, Jane O'Reilly, Joan Platt and Zoe.

Birth was the death of me. Downhill ever since.
—*Samuel Beckett*

"No" is the wildest word in the English language.
—*Emily Dickinson*

Part I

Intro

In 1948 some lotus seeds were found twenty feet beneath the earth near Tokyo. Scientists calculated the carbon 14 content of the seeds and said they were more than three thousand years old. Strange to say, when the stone-hard husks of the seeds were filed away and the seeds themselves were allowed to lie free on wet cotton, they sprouted. Planted in the bed of a shallow pool, they grew and blossomed.

What I wondered, when I read about the lotus seeds in the Apachanack Community Library in Whitby Cove—this was a year or so after Eliza was born—what I wondered was, was it very clear when the filing-away was taking place, were the scientists sure, which was seed and which was husk?

Because it struck me that life was jammed inside those lotus seeds in much the same way life jams together in a family. In a family, the husband, the wife, the child, the father, the mother, the daughter, are like objects brought so close that all the edges blur. Ghosts of old selves resurface, fuse into others. It is even sometimes hard to tell what parts contain life and what parts are dead, so seamlessly does one build from the other, life on death and death on life.

When he was past eighty and getting ready to die, Jung remarked that the only events of his life worth telling were the moments when the imperishable erupted into the transitory world. Life, he said, had always seemed like a plant to him, a plant that lives on something called rhizome. A rhizome is the thick stem under the soil that produces roots belowground and shoots aboveground. A plant's source, its true life, is hidden in its rhizome. We see only the part of the plant that grows and flowers and detaches but not what feeds the flowering or remains belowground after the flowering.

Loosely speaking, "family rhizome" is the lump of a name I'd give to all that invisible stuff you can't get hold of. It's that place of fluid friction where the "grand" forces battle each other. Desire is in there, and fear.

Family rhizome has got to have some odd properties. For example, it has to have the capacity to both attract and repel. It must be attractive enough to compel new life out of amorphous being and repellent enough to push that life away into its own separate being.

In the plant world, the germ of life can remain in the world of the living dead for a very long time (over three thousand years). Similarly, like those lotus seeds, some hearts do try to stay hidden within the husk of the family. This is true of children and also true of adults who enter marriage still dreaming the dream of protection. I cannot be separate anymore or again, they think. It will lead to the end of me.

They are right, of course, but what then? Being right is of no use here. The act of thinking is itself separation. No sooner do we think than we distance ourselves from what we are thinking about. The life of the individual has begun.

I never knew what the others thought or what they liked thinking about or what they were thinking when they talked. But I want to tell you a story about the year our family fell apart, at least where the plant or the flowering, what any one of us could see, fell apart. So I'll have to tell it to you from my own point of view. From my point of view, this is a love story. A love story that starts with death.

*T*he first news about how sick Benjamin's mother was came from Mrs. Spencer. Mrs. Spencer is the head of Coventry School, where my daughter Eliza is, so a call from her has the effect of a good alarm clock. In this case, she took the time, highly unusual, to personally telephone each kindergarten mother. Measuring her voice with deliberate and frequent pauses, she explained that Benjamin had told the entire class that morning that his mother was dying. Apparently Chuck Dover, Benjamin's father, brought him to school and the two of them talked with the teacher about it first. Benjamin said then that he didn't want to tell the children yet, but he did want to be in school. However, about twenty minutes later, when it was Benjamin's turn for show-and-tell, he stood and said that his mother had cancer and she had been operated on but the operation hadn't worked.

Mrs. Spencer went on about show-and-tell. She said it was a time for the children to "share" some news, something that happened over the weekend, something meaningful to them. In other words, Benjamin's decision to talk about his mother had been perfectly appropriate, but it had come as a surprise, and Eliza might have some thoughts or questions about it when she got home. (What I like about Coventry School is that they take my daughter as seriously as I do.)

Later on, the class mother called and told me more. The children had asked Benjamin only a few questions about his mother. One child wanted to know why the doctors didn't give her different medicine and Benjamin said they had no more medicine to give. Another child asked what day she was going to die and Benjamin said, "On Christmas."

"In the morning or the afternoon?" one of the boys wanted to know.

"In the morning," said Benjamin, adding, "I think." He wasn't sure because his mother was always in her pajamas. It always seemed like morning.

I turned on the computer and went back to work. I'm not usually too busy—I make sure of that because I want to keep time for Eliza—but I had some mangled sentences I had to get straight by the next morning. I write public relations copy for a brokerage firm. It's odd work. My job is to rewrite the reports of the financial analysts in the global-risk-management department. The main advantage to this job is that I get to work at home most of the time. But sometimes the work itself is just impossible. It was that day. I would have given something very important to me, probably a new towel, to anyone who had come along and helped me rewrite this sentence: "Mortgage investors who bought yield-curve notes a few years ago were burned by negative convexity." Sometimes my job isn't impossible at all, if I can just remember that everybody has risk strategies. Some apply them to money and some apply them to people.

Risk management is a way to play safe by building yourself safety nets. It teaches a life lesson I don't like knowing or learning. Calculated risk is the only sane way to live a life. I almost don't even want to be reckless anymore, that's how well I've internalized my job. Anyway, mothers can't afford to be radicals. Radicals commit crimes and have to leave their children and go to jail.

To let you in early on my character, I am a calculating person and I am a selfish person. I am, for example, selfish about sheets and towels. I have a whole closetful of new sheets and towels. I never offer the new ones to guests and I don't put them out for Hank and not for myself either. Eliza has great towels, and when they get just a little bit scratchy I move them into our bathroom for Hank and me and I put out new ones for her. I realize that giving her new towels is the same as giving myself new towels (Hank has pointed this out to me).

When Eliza got off the bus at four o'clock that day, I said, "Tell me one thing that happened in school today."

"Katie S. brought her frog in for show-and-tell. Mom, why can't I have a frog?" She pushed back her moppy hair and she started making noise from deep in her throat. "See, I already know how to talk to them."

"What do frogs eat?" I said.

"Worms. Live ones."

"Only live ones?"

"Yeah. They can't be dead. Frogs don't eat anything dead."

"I don't think the city is a good place for a frog," I said.

"Maybe they can eat flies too," she offered, expertly picking up on the point of resistance. I told her we would talk about it later.

I brought up the subject that evening when Hank came home. He was late as usual. He teaches a seminar on global finance strategies on Tuesday to bank trainees, and they always keep him after class. I was in the green chair in the kitchen, peeling an orange. He reached for a double section and I stopped him. "That's for Eliza's breakfast tomorrow. I'm saving it. Sorry."

I put a banana in front of him and I told him about Benjamin's mother's dying.

"Do you know her?" he asked me.

"No, except by sight. Benjamin is new this year and Eliza has only been to his house once. The housekeeper was there when I picked her up."

"Does Eliza know her?"

"She hasn't said anything about her."

"Well, don't worry. Death isn't frightening to children. It's interesting to them."

"You can't mean that the way it sounds."

"Sure. Children are realists. Besides, it won't be a problem for Eliza if it's not a problem for Benjamin. And it won't be a problem for Benjamin."

"It won't be a problem for Benjamin?"

"No, it won't. It's the father that boys really need. Besides, children can be imprinted like ducks. You could teach Benjamin a steam shovel was his mother. Look at you."

This is true. In a way. My mother, Alice Yarmouth, died when I was an infant and my aunt raised me. I always called my aunt Mom, mostly because her name was Kate and my name is Kate and it was confusing. But also because I never think of Alice as a bona fide mother. She was much younger than my aunt, and when my aunt talked about her sister, Alice, I got a picture of a girl not yet allowed to cross the street by herself. I said, "My aunt was not a steam shovel."

"I'm just making a point, Kate."

"I know what you're doing," I said. I went on to the frog. I said I thought we should get one. It couldn't be such a big deal. It would only eat flies. And Eliza seemed so interested in them and she really did sound like a frog when she imitated one. (I was in the abstract favorable to frogs because my aunt knew frog stories that helped me. Once when I was having trouble in geometry, for example, she told me about the two frogs who fell into a big milk vat. When they swam to the top and realized their predicament, one frog gave up and sank to the bottom and drowned. But the other frog kept swimming. He kept swimming till he thought his little legs would give out. After a good long while he felt something hard underneath him and he crouched stock-still and discovered he had made butter and he didn't have to swim one more stroke.)

Hank raised his chin and smiled. "I get it. Bravo! You will spend the weekends in Central Park catching flies for your daughter, and you will watch her feed them to her frog, with whom she will have important, throaty conversations. Great idea, Kate!" He gave a little chuckle and shook his large head and reached for my shirt, pulling it to point out a stain on the side, and ate half of Eliza's orange because he knew I wouldn't dare stop him a second time.

I often pleaded ridiculous things on behalf of Eliza. My idea about her was that I wanted to give her the world and then I wanted to climb into it with her. It was all wrong. I knew it was wrong, and I kept trying to stop being so tied in to her. It was hard. I thought about things only in relation to her, and she was the only thing I could think to talk to Hank about.

It hadn't always been like that. Before Eliza was born, it was worse.

You could say our marriage was like the telephone cord in the kitchen. Part of it twisted one way and the other part the opposite way. I never could figure out how to get both sides going the same way or how it got like that in the first place.

I knew a few things. Hank and I weren't in love by the time we married, though there had been an initial spark. There had been a spark.

It happened during the short time I spent as Hank's student, the briefest and to date the sexiest bit of our time together. I was new at the bank and I was in one of his training seminars. He was an unusual person in that he had refused to give up his crew cut even though his hair had gone gray. It gave him a wounded look and certainly got my attention. I sat in the front of the class, watching him stalk back and forth, big head, big eyes, clean-cut mouth, thinking out loud about options and futures and contracts and presenting them like gifts. "An option," he said, in his clear, banging voice fairly early on, "gives the holder a right to do something. For example," and he surged up to me from across the room, "if I ask you to marry me, Miss Yarmouth, I am giving you an option on my life." He paused as if hit by a stun gun and stood for a time in front of me. The only thing stirring in his massive form was his forehead, which was furrowing and unfurrowing. It took a moment but he continued: "You do not have to exercise your option, Miss Yarmouth. Of course. But perhaps my example will help you remember the crucial distinction between options and futures: The holder of an option does not, I repeat, does not, have to exercise the option, whereas the holder of a futures contract is obligated to buy or sell the underlying asset."

Then he crossed back to the blackboard in two strides, turned his powerful face once more to me, and addressed us all: "If anyone forgets or has a problem with what is an option and what is a futures contract, you need only ask Miss Yarmouth. I assure you she will be able to tell you."

It was a crackling encounter in my life, and in his too, I imagined. Neither one of us was the least bit surprised when I showed up at his office asking for help on a problem the next day, or that we never discussed that problem, or that, though he was an expert, I hardly ever asked him again to explain about risk-neutral valuation or anything else with a Greek letter in it and minus and plus and equal signs and T for Time and small t for a different kind of time. And when we discovered he was from the Connecticut town I was born in but never grew up in, well, it seemed like fate. There was even the further coincidence that our names were also the names of streets in town, he told me. Willoughby Street ran into Yarmouth Avenue at the town firehouse. Again, it was destiny, as far as you could reckon destiny in the 1980s.

All that initial excitement stayed at the bank, however, and I, the new Mrs. Willoughby, stayed at home.

We thought the fact that we were level-headed about each other was probably a good thing because, as Hank said, until we met, I hadn't had any valid opportunity to let love grow on me. I've always liked men. I like their breathlessness, their skin, their heat, lots of things about them. Hank said that what I had with men before he came along was precisely that, a life of the skin, a coating of flattery and excitement. With not one of them could I have put down roots.

Men for me, before Hank, were connected with sports, and that may have had something to do with my father, whom I never met and who is a total mystery to me, as I would be to him because he didn't even know about me. I never knew who he was because my mother never named him to her sister or to anybody else, or me to him. My mother was probably about two weeks pregnant when lightning hit the golf pro shop owned by her parents. Both parents were instantly killed, which left my mother in the care of my aunt, who was twelve years older than she was. My aunt sent my mother East to the summer house of distant relatives, who were in Italy that year, while she reorganized the pro shop.

My aunt used to say my father must have been a tennis player, because I have a knack for the game, and I have somebody else's constitution, I think, or my aunt said so, certainly not that of my delicate, frail mother, whose weak heart gave out three days after I was born. My aunt took me home from the hospital and renamed me Kate (the women in the Yarmouth family are all either Kate or Alice and for three days I had been Alice).

From the very beginning I was at the pro shop all hours of the day and night, and later I was still there, because we lived on the club grounds. My aunt said I went from bottles to boys on tennis courts, and that must have been at least partly true, because as a girl, until I moved East to college because my aunt insisted I get to know a city to prepare me for life on my own, sex to me was all about boys in tennis shorts.

In these times it would be reasonable to ask why I

hadn't tried to go on in tennis instead of watching boys who played tennis. I guess the quick answer is, I wasn't good enough, and the longer answer is also, I wasn't good enough.

Meantime, all my boys and men were what Hank called False Relations—intimations of, flirtations with, the Real Thing. The Real Thing was something organic. The fact that I didn't have any automatic feeling for Hank going into the marriage was fine with him. "Good," he said. Because love is organic, something that grows best in the hothouse of marriage. Married love is cultivated love, a deep folding, and melding, and blending. I thought he knew. He was old and wise, and he adored me, he said. I didn't see why I couldn't develop something organic with him, someone who adored me, who wanted to make a life of deep folds, left his wife to make a life of deep folds, with me.

I waited to feel the leafy pleasure I thought should accompany deep folding. But there wasn't any. In fact, there was no folding. The time we spent together as man and wife was as disconnected moment-to-moment as the jumps on a digital clock. We had the busy-ness of his family, his career, my work, dinners, friends. We went to and gave many costume parties and played English charades, and that seemed like fun, sort of. We also had the busy-ness of slightly making me over, which always struck me as more quaint than anything else, and which

I took to be the measure of the almost thirteen years between us. Hank liked to dress me and order clothes for me, principally nightgowns and white nothings of cotton lace or trimmed with cotton lace. He threw away my boat shoes and my jeans. He changed my part from the side to the middle and asked me to grow my hair long. He shopped antique stores and sent home a vanity and a big old-fashioned mirror, in which he liked to look at my reflection, he said. He wanted me to have things, "woman's things," body lotion, hand cream, special soap for sensitive skin. Our first argument was over the fact that I did not collect and display feminine accoutrements in the private places in our house. He was partial to Chanel, to Chanel perfume and "nude" cosmetics, and I ended up with so many pale lipsticks and brushes and blushers and powders and creams and soaps one would have thought there were six or seven of me.

On the whole, all our activity seemed newlywed-appropriate. We took up each other's time in ways I had imagined we would and we had few complaints about each other.

What bothered Hank about me was so quirky that it didn't bother me. For example, he absolutely didn't like my thumbs. It's a fact that they are flat and rather wide, but it struck me as overdoing it when he reminded me to cover them up whenever pictures of us, or me, were taken. I figured thumbs had some erotic significance peculiar to his generation and my thumbs were gross and frontal and offensive to him.

What bothered me about Hank was that he lied about weird things. He lied, for example, about his age. He said he was two years younger than he actually was. It was an open lie in that he laughed about it when corrected. But he wouldn't stop, and when I asked him why he lied about his age, he said he wanted to be two years younger. He said it in a voice that could have been his when he was three years old and believed he was whatever he wanted to be. The lie was a hopeless, silly, naked thing, a small thing, the sort of thing that could create a soft affection for him, the kind I felt, for example, when he maintained he was wearing socks when he wasn't or when I saw him tucking the extra skin from his neck into his collar, a habitual gesture. But it could also give off a sense, to me, that the ground we stood on together was less firm than it appeared.

Hank liked to garden. I would have thought gardening was something to do when you're old or after your knees give out, but since Hank didn't play tennis, I gardened with him at his country place in Whitby Cove. He liked to teach and he taught me a lot. Some of it was awfully nice, especially in the beginning. He began by interesting me in catalogs, then in dirt, and when I showed weakness there, consigned me to the raking and care and repair of the brick paths and to blasting the roses with the hose to wash off the aphids on the buds. I learned that water, just water, kills soft-bodied insects. It was somehow clear, though, right from the beginning, that there wasn't going to be much togetherness in gardening together. It wasn't, it didn't ever have the feel of, shared activity. It was more like division of labor.

The best job I had was the lilacs. When I first saw the lilac bushes I thought they were trees. They were over twenty feet tall and they bloomed out of a tangle of honeysuckle and brier. My job was to trim the spent blossoms off the branches. I went at it with a pair of super-duper loppers one weekend when Hank was at a conference and I wanted to surprise him with my enthusiasm. The result was that I had this job only one season because I overtrimmed (Hank says "scalped") the bushes and we had no blossoms for the next two years.

By that time, Hank was into very complicated stuff, ecosystems and bird and bug habits and habitats, and getting involved was harder for me than trying to enter a double-Dutch jump rope game. I quit. Hank seemed more relieved than anything else, but it puzzled him, he said. I felt ashamed, as if not wanting to garden were an indication that I did not have normal human equipment, which his puzzlement seemed to imply. He shook his head over it for about a year or so.

When I stopped gardening I began to notice that in

the part of married life that is supposed to just "happen," nothing had happened. We didn't have any of those spontaneous small noticings that mean everything in the end because they sink to the core, and when they come up again, in the middle of something else, putting on the left-turn signal or washing under one arm in the shower, they come up all fused, you and your chosen one and what the two of you noticed together. We had, instead, blank spots. Things that might have been between us were not between us, were without connections, because we missed opportunities to say something, to remark on them, one to the other, to connect the little things to both of us. More and more our marriage seemed to amount to an accumulation of lipsticks and blanks.

It almost seemed as if the blanks were real, real lost things, losses that ought to be visible, or at least measurable, if not in themselves, then in their effect on us. Something like Benjamin's mother, I guess. She was going to be definitely gone. Things were going to happen to her, and to Benjamin.

Hank wasn't keen on having children. He said he had to deal with enough children in his life (he was the eldest of seven) and at the bank, including me, though I was no longer working at the bank, of course. He had been firm about that with his first wife, but I must have been more tenacious. I justified pushing for a baby by reasoning it would help if I could see Hank in a child. He might be less remote to me. So Eliza, bless her small violent heart, was born, a live, bloody, screaming thing. Into a dormant marriage.

The first day we spent the whole afternoon in the hospital together, holding her, mostly Hank was holding her. He kept his hospital gown on every moment because he was so often cradling her in his outsized arms.

I happened to have with me a book called *The Rights of Infants,* and from it I explained to Hank that his holding her was helping her learn how to breathe. Her first cry was actually an emergency form of breathing, because breathing wasn't a habit yet with her. She didn't know how to do it; moreover she wasn't developed enough to do it easily. We had to help her along. Get her into the habit. And the way to do that was to do exactly what he was doing, hold her.

I read to him as he held her: " 'The prenatal baby, having no access to the outer air, breathes from the placenta through the blood. This ration becomes scant as her nervous system matures. Blood analysis shows that the baby, somewhat like a person living at an extremely high altitude, endures a condition of progressive oxygen privation. . . .

" 'Handling initiates deeper inspiration and helps in its establishment. From being held, fondled, allowed to

suck freely and frequently, the child receives reflex stim-
ulation which primes the breathing mechanism into action and which finally enables the whole respiratory
process to become organized under the control of the
baby's own nervous system.'

"You are teaching her how to breathe," I told him.

"You're exaggerating," he said. He rearranged her
blanket and held her more closely.

We were a family until I left the hospital and Hank
went back to work. From then on, it was just Eliza and
me. Hank had been right, one hundred percent. The real
thing *was* organic, and it seemed to have nothing to do
with him.

And everything that wasn't part of what was organic,
what wasn't Eliza and me, was completely superfluous.

In a way I had been prepared for Eliza. I was expect-
ing something overwhelming and obsessive, like the
opening weeks of falling in love. She surprised me,
though. We had that and then we had that and then we
had that. It was continuous. It was flat-out exhausting
and there was no end. I could not pay attention to
anything else, could not pay attention to anything at all
for longer than a minute, including Eliza, but that was
the limit she set. Speaking for the both of us, I'd say we
were a desperate pair. There was an undertow between
us, so that I felt drowned alternately by waves of love
and hate and jealousy and by fear that I was losing my

own mind. I felt that every fiber of mine was connected to her, and I sometimes wanted at any cost to be free of her and rest again in my old solitary self, knowing I would claw apart anything that loomed in her horizon and might possibly divert her from the physical and emotional longing that delivered us to each other and blurred all boundaries between us.

Eliza and I were so much a unit that I often had to kick my shin under the table so I didn't cry out in alarm when I heard the key turning in the door at night and Hank came in as if it was where he belonged.

It sounds as if I were making a joke about it. I am not making a joke about it. It is an agony not to love the man you live with. You hate yourself.

Some things just can't grow into each other and make something bigger. Our marriage was one of those things, a grafting job that just didn't take, any more than Hank's attempt to meld a dwarf apple with a crab apple tree did that first spring. I finally had to accept that I just couldn't love him, though I couldn't think of one blessed reason not to love him. I just didn't. That was it. It was not something I could tell him, either, of course, any more than he could show me the withered roots of the tree he dug up on a June night when he thought I was taking a shower. I let the water run and watched him.

So at the end of the day, here we were, parents and

child, not husband and wife. She was the link between us, what, besides the fact that we all lived in the same house, proved our existence as a unit. She was more a receptacle than anything else, a whatnot basket for the mangled wishes and hopes of her parents. And she had about as much chance of growing out of the whatnot soil she was rooted in as a tree in sidewalk does.

The guilt that says "I caused this" is better, more tolerable, than the helplessness that says "It has nothing to do with me." The truth is, I don't feel guilty. I feel sorry, sorry that I don't love him and sorry that I'm afraid to say "I do not love you." It was such a relief to fall in love with Eliza, and maybe that's why I cannot let her go. And also, I guess, why I never talked to Hank about how moist and boneless and delicate she felt to me when I carried her around, or what passed through my head and body whenever I heard her small noises, or the happiness it was to be in her company even, at times especially, when she slept.

Anyway, I've come to believe that parents are there to protect the children. It's right that the attachment between mothers and their children is so strong, stronger than that between husband and wife. If the wife's strongest bond was her husband, and the children were somewhere outside her passion, you could get a gang-up situation that puts the child outside the loop with no protector. You could get a situation like Lisa Steinberg's, whose drugged parents beat her senseless just after Halloween a few years ago. She died.

I can hear Hank now: "Stop being dramatic."

Okay.

Benjamin came over to play a few days before the end of school. The children leapt off the bus. Eliza embraced me around the waist, her hair a tangle and her eyes black and bright. "Mom," she said, "can Benjamin sleep over around Christmas, because his mother is going to die then, and I think he might feel uncomfortable."

"No, no," said Benjamin. We were in the elevator by then. "I'm having a party that day. I'm inviting everyone in my class, and you too." He poked Eliza in the chest for emphasis when he said the word "you."

Benjamin had a shopping bag full of things he was bringing home from his cubby at school. He brought it to the table and put it next to his chair. He reached in and pulled out a picture in an oval silver frame. "This is my mother," he said. In the picture, Benjamin's mother wore cutoffs and a tie-dyed T-shirt. She had light hair and it fell long and straight. There was a red-and-yellow baseball cap on top of her head. Benjamin said his mother used to be a pitcher for her softball team in Somerville, but you couldn't tell that now because she had no hair and she couldn't wear her hat. He caught me staring at him, so he went on: "It slides down over her eyes," he said by way of explanation.

Benjamin looked at the picture while he ate his chicken noodle soup. Eliza read a book out loud about Frog and Toad being friends forever. Then she and Benjamin built houses out of blocks for Eliza's new frog and put the frog through its paces, having it try out all the rooms.

After I took Benjamin home in the late afternoon, I happened upon his mother sunning on a park bench across the street. The incidental motion that caught my attention might have been a light adjustment to her wig. Now her hands were resting in her lap and her chin was stretching up toward the sun. She wore no lipstick, but her nails were painted in the manner of a French manicure, so that the body of the nail looked naked and naturally buffed while the tips were chalk white. She had a faint smile. There was a dappled look about her figure on the bench, insubstantial and tentative, but she herself appeared limpid and calm. With her eyes closed, her face had the quality of a water-smoothed stone. She is going to die without wrinkles, I thought, and I crossed the street to her, interrupting her sun as I passed in front of her.

She felt me sit down beside her and blinked, so that the pale disk of her face broke apart. I saw that she did not at first recognize me without the attachment of

Eliza, but then I saw that she did. "I love the sun too," I said.

"Uumnnn," she said.

"I just dropped off Benj," I said.

"Benjamin," she corrected. Next to me now, she seemed a lot smaller than average, though I am five foot nine and it's hard to judge. There was an old-fashioned, powdery, perfume smell about her that reminded me of long ago, of my mother on her porch, though this could not have been a real memory, as my mother had died so early on. It had to have been my aunt's porch, her iced tea, her long silver straws, her papery legs, her bare feet up on the cracked flowery cushions, that I was seeing through Benjamin's mother, though that didn't click either. A movie, maybe, or a wish. "Mrs. Dover," I said.

"Isabel, please," she said. "Thank you for taking Benjamin today. He's crazy about Eliza. Did they have fun?" She shut her eyes and her face reverted to eggshell.

"Isabel," I began again. "I'm Kate."

"I've been taking lessons," she said. "I actually go to a school to learn how to let go. My husband goes too. He has to learn to let go of me. He's not facing it. He won't give up. He wants to move us all to Arizona. He wants me to have another operation."

"You go to school?"

"Benjamin calls it the Good-bye School. It's group therapy."

Quiet. The light on her face was even now.

"It must be terrifying to think of letting Benjamin go," I said.

"No. It isn't."

Quiet.

"It isn't?"

"No. Not now. When Benjamin was a baby it was hard. Now he's doing it all by himself. All I have to do is let him."

"I should go to your school. Sometimes I feel like a criminal, holding on to Eliza the way I do."

"In a way you probably are. It's exclusive, anyway. Not good for either of you."

I felt an urge to take out my brush and have a show-off go at my hair. Instead I said, "That's it. Exclusive. *Criminal*'s an exaggeration."

"But it's not up to you. You know that, right? It's almost over. It's already over."

For you, maybe, I thought. I lapsed into an internal scuffle. She was so high-handed, but I was the one who had sought her out in the first place. I wanted something from her, and she was dying, and after all, she hadn't said, Don't bother me, I have cancer. I could at least listen to her and stop talking to myself.

Isabel's eyes were on me. She said, "Surely, you two don't have the same intensity you had together when she was born."

I had to admit we didn't. Or Eliza didn't. I said, "I don't know if she does but I do. A lot of the time I do. I'm so attached to her still, through habit, maybe, or guilt. I am always, always wondering if I am doing what is right for her, if I'm doing enough for her. I'm at the limit of my nerves with her." (What does this mean? I thought.) "Most of the time."

"Don't worry. You'll grow out of it."

"That is exactly what worries me. I don't want to grow out of it."

"You'll have to. They start to move away from you. You think you can never let them go, and then they do it all by themselves. One day they look beyond you and they see that the world is bigger than you and that's what they have to go for. Then they start arching their backs away from you. Nothing personal."

(Whatever you say, your majesty.) "I guess not. It feels personal. Did you learn that at school?"

"No," she said. She laughed. "I learned it when he did it," she said.

I didn't like being laughed at but I truly didn't want to leave her, maybe because she was still holding all the cards or maybe because these were things I would have tried to puzzle out with my own mother if she had grown up, or with Hank if he were into puzzling, which he definitely wasn't. "I'll tell you how I feel about Eliza," I said. I was leaning toward her, trying to make her not close her eyes again. "I look at Eliza and I am looking at the source of my strength. It's because of her that I have any self-discipline at all, any patience, any willingness to be bored, to wipe her chin again and again, to go for a slow walk, to call those small times life, which they are, to me. A great wide life." (I believed this.)

"She should be wiping her own chin by now," Isabel said.

"She is." (Most of the time.)

Pause. I didn't want this to end. Think, Kate, quickly. I told her about our platform bed, how after I was first married and before Eliza was born, I used to hide things in the square hollow over which the platform rested, and then the mattress and then the sheets and covers and comforters and pillows. This hiding habit led to constant dismantling, both to put things in and later to look for things I had put in for safekeeping. I just kept taking that bed apart. I'd be frantic to find a photograph, a leaf, a piece of paper with an important message on it. Sometimes I would find what I was looking for. It would be a stone with a pattern or a scrap with three or four words running together, sometimes lovely-sounding, sometimes ridiculous, sometimes abstractly interesting. The consistency was that no matter what the phrase or the token was that once reeked with significance, now it meant nothing. "After Eliza was born," I said, "I stopped taking the bed apart and I have never felt the need to take it apart since."

"Eliza turned out to be what you lost," Isabel said.

"Somehow. I'm trying not to cross over to the freaky."

"You have to be careful, Kate," Isabel said, "and this is something I did learn in school. You have to be careful with Eliza so you don't wind up using her to feel strong yourself." She saw the "huh?" in my face. She added: "She'll never be able to give you up if you need her to be weak."

"Part of me knows this," I said. "But it's not easy to order myself around. Listen, excuse me for complaining." She waved her hand, excusing me.

"You know what I loved about my baby, when Benjamin was a baby. I loved watching him wake up, all his little baby senses plowing the air, just desperate to touch base again with the world."

"Right," I said. I knew this from my reading. Babies fall asleep and wake up about forty-five times a day and each time the world is completely new to them. It's because they don't have any habits and because they're so dependent. Every time they fall asleep and wake up they have to learn everything all over again. They do it or they don't survive.

"Well, now, I keep fading in and out and having to start over. In that sense, Benjamin and I are reversed almost. It's strange."

"I think I know what you mean. Say it again."

But she was tired. Her eyes closed down. She was her own island, insubstantial and gentle island of peach-down cheeks and smooth square brow. She sighed with her whole chest. "The good thing about all this is that it's made me get rid of all the bullshit in my life," she said.

Quiet.

"What's one example of bullshit?" I said.

"Bullshit," she said.

"You're funny, Isabel," I said.

"You too," she said.

On the day before Coventry closed for the summer, the parents were invited to the final lower school assembly. Eliza wanted to go by herself on the school bus and I took her down in the elevator. On the way, she asked me, "If you're deaf, can you still speak?"

"No," I said.

"Can you move?"

"No."

"Can you see?"

"No."

"Why not?"

"Because when you die, the brain and heart die. They are the life of the body, and that makes the body die and not be able to speak or move."

"Not dying. Death."

"Death is what happens when you die."

"Not death. DEAF."

"Oh, I misunderstood you. Let's start again. No, you can't hear if you're deaf, but you can move and see and speak. Sometimes, it's hard for a deaf person to learn how to speak because he can't hear the words and repeat them, and sometimes people have trouble understanding him."

Hank showed up just then and the bus came and Eliza got on and waved with both hands, and then we were lucky and caught a cab and arrived in time for the traditional ceremony in which all the children are promoted by acclamation: "Kindergarten students, you are now first graders!" said Mrs. Spencer and our class stood up and cheered. The cheers got louder and stronger until the fourth graders, who were now fifth graders, shrieked and howled and cried, "I can't believe I'm in the fifth grade!" And there was clapping and rejoicing all around.

The mother next to me, whom I didn't recognize, took my hand and squeezed it. "They made it," she said. Her tears fell on my hand.

"They're great," I said.

Then came a concert and a procession. Off to one side, children holding bells in their white-gloved hands stood, two to a music stand, looking intently at the music and shaking the bells. The littlest children started singing a song about being "over the meadow, green and wide," and the slightly older ones, some of them whistling, joined in as they lined up in pairs facing each other so that two parallel lines of older children gradually built up from the piano on the far side of the gym to the exit door near the lunchroom. The older ones carried colored ribbons and each gave one end to his partner, so that four hands, holding the ends of bright streamers, rose simultaneously in the air, and four hands after that, and on and on until there was an archway of children and ribbons spanning the breadth of the gym. Then the littlest ones, our little ones, who were still singing "over the meadow, green and wide, blooming in the sunlight, blooming in the sun-un light," began to walk under the archway of ribbons and then soon they were out the door, noisily and triumphantly climbing the stairs to their classrooms, where they sat for the last time in their kindergarten chairs and peeled the lids off the Dixie cups in front of them and ate vanilla ice cream with flat wooden spoons.

Teary mothers stood looking at each other as if to ask, Why are we crying?

Maybe we were crying for the songs we never sang or

the ribbons we never walked under. But what, years from now, would make our children cry when they saw their own children? And how could we prevent it?

That night I dreamed about Isabel and me. We were schoolmates in Benjamin's Good-bye School.

The director told me I would be there a long, long time. She said I was so far behind the others that the chances were slim that I would ever catch up. She said she had agreed to take me only on Isabel's recommendation. Isabel had convinced her that I would be an interesting challenge. She sent me home to pack my suitcase, and when I came back she confiscated it, claiming she had to sort out the extraneous things I had brought with me.

There was a prayer over the entrance to the Good-bye School:

Do not take a stand against reality.

Do not hold that the object in fact cannot be lost.

Withdraw from a lost and irretrievable object.

The director said I was to copy this prayer and keep it in my pocket and consult it often. Then she hung a sandwich sign around my neck so that the same message appeared to those seeing me from behind or coming toward me. It said: WATCH OUT! MY OBJECTIVE IS LETHAL FUSION.

My spot at school was next to Isabel because I was

the newest and she was the one closest to graduation. We (there were so many of us) slept in a long, hollow room with cots in it. White iron cots. The ceiling was the height of a gymnasium. The radiators were uncovered. They hissed. We had to make our beds with hospital corners. There was no fuzz under my bed and there was to be no fuzz.

There were speakers on the bedposts. They announced inspection times in quadraphonics. I learned that I had arrived just in time for an inspection but with not enough time to get ready for it. I slid under the bed to check for fuzz. I decided to stay under the bed.

But Isabel coaxed me and I agreed to get out. I got caught on part of the bed frame. Isabel unhooked me. "It's all right," she said. "I am with you. You will get all the help you need."

The path to the refectory was a maze and the maze changed before every meal. The idea was to leave the old path behind and constantly find a new way. Trying to remember the old path did no good. In fact it hindered finding the new path.

Over the refectory was written: "Deference to reality gains the day." We were obliged to read it aloud before entering. If a student forgot to read it, she had to go back and start again. A new maze, of course.

Eliza was allowed to visit me every day. She sat at my knee to receive instruction in the art of losing. In fact,

*the only way I could get out of the school was by
proving I had learned the good-bye lessons. The proof
was that when I taught my daughter, she believed me.
She laughed and laughed.*

*But Isabel was sympathetic. "You'll get another
chance tomorrow," she said.*

Later that week Isabel Dover telephoned and said Benjamin really wanted Eliza to sleep at his house that night instead of the other way round, the way we had originally planned it, and would it be all right. I said, "Of course, if you want to have her." (When do you stop being normal with someone who is dying?) So Eliza packed up and I took her over. Isabel answered the door in a silk robe and dark lipstick. Her head was completely bald and shiny on the top. She apologized for not having a wig on and I said, "It must feel cool" (we were in the grip of a scorcher day), and she said, "Yes, it feels cool."

She invited me in.

A fan blew over a picture on the hall table and I picked it up. It was Baby Benjamin, nose to nose with a puppy. She took the picture and set it straight and remarked: "When I was pregnant with Benjamin, I felt like we were a miracle." She told me how she admired Benjamin's body, its slenderness and softness and grace, his suppleness, which she feared might disappear.

"I first felt him as something liquid, I think. We were trying to remember that in therapy yesterday. There was a sensation, a rumble in me, coming through many layers. I didn't hear it exactly. I felt it. It was a subtle thing. I remember thinking, This is life, this is muscle in the making."

I thought, It's too bad only dying people are allowed to talk like that. Even vicariously it was a release for me, like undoing the top button on my skirt, which I managed just then, surreptitiously, I hoped. "I had a dream about your therapy," I said. And I told her.

"It can't hurt to be prepared," she said.

"I hope your therapy lasts forever," I said.

"Lethal fusion is a funny idea," Isabel said.

"Not funny to the object," I said.

"Don't blow yourself up, Kate. You're not that powerful."

"Good," I said.

"There is one thing, though," said Isabel. She was moving around her apartment, straightening, picking up balls and plastic bats and rackets. I was following her.

"What?" I said.

"Catch," she said. She threw a nerf ball at me.

"This is my favorite game," I said.

"What I was going to say is"—we were throwing the

ball back and forth—"I thought of it after our conversation the other day. Sometimes when you love children or animals too much, you love them against something. You want to be careful about that. It's no good for anybody."

"Love them against whom?" I said.

"I don't know. Whoever else is in your life."

The ball hit my nose.

"Bull's-eye," said Isabel. Then, "As long as you're feeling helpful, let's make the bed," she said. We went into her room and began pulling and pushing the sheets. We were happy together. We were two women who believed that mothers have a lock on the ultimate human experience. Our smugness and assurance came from this one thing, and our guilt came from this also, as well as our feeling that, except between us, we had to hide our satisfaction so as not to arouse the jealousy of those who could not have babies. We got the bed made in no time, at which point Benjamin and Eliza came whooping in and Benjamin jumped on it.

Isabel said, "You're just doing that because you think I'll let you do anything."

"Yep," he said. "Come on, Eliza."

"It's okay, Eliza," said Isabel.

So Eliza climbed on too and announced she and Benjamin had a joke for us.

"What's the joke?" I said.

"First we need to ask you a lot of questions about your memory," said Benjamin.

"Oh, this is a good one," said Isabel. "Do it for Eliza's mom."

So they did. First they took turns, testing my memory.

"Will you remember me a second from now?"

"Yes."

"A minute from now?"

"Yes."

"An hour?"

"Yes."

"A month?"

"A year?"

"Ten years from now?"

"Of course," I said.

"Great," said Benjamin. "Okay, Eliza, you take over."

"Okay," said Eliza. "Knock, knock."

"Who's there?" I said.

"You don't remember me?" said Eliza. Her eyes were wide open and her hands loose at her sides.

Pause. Everybody else laughed and then I laughed.

"Good, huh?" said Benjamin. "See you guys later. Come on, Eliza."

They left and Isabel returned my stare. "How can you stand to hear that?" I said.

"How can I not," she answered.

She stood up and I stood up and we went toward the door. She said she was going to give the children soda with their dinner because they had been promoted and deserved special treats. There would be *pain au chocolat* for breakfast too, which she pronounced as if it were English, "pain-oh-chocolate." I asked her if she was in pain and she said she wasn't. She was just waiting. The wait was so long, she said. Her eyes were clear and her look was still and steady. Then she said, "It wasn't enough," and turned to shut the door.

"Your life," I said to her back. I saw that on the nape of her neck there was still a bit of straggly hair. I put my hand on her back. Her wing bones stuck out. "I'm sorry," I said.

"Not enough," she answered, still not turning around.

I took a step closer to her and I put my arms all the way around her. I made her an island again. She was more delicate than Humpty-Dumpty. I said, still to her back, "Can I do something for you?"

"Thank you. I know you want to do something. I will call you if there is something."

I kissed the back of her bald head. "You have courage, Isabel," I said.

"Thank you," she answered and closed her door.

• • •

There were no more return dates for a while.

Both children spent the summer outside the city. In the country, in Whitby Cove, Eliza worried for a while about who had hair and who didn't. She noticed Hank had very little hair, and I think that upset Hank more than it did her. She decided she would grow her own hair very long, and she seemed to forget about Benjamin and his mother.

It happened that at the time Hank was interested in death too, in an intriguing, if quirky, way, involving visits to a couple of Connecticut graveyards and some photographing. He was trying to arrange for his grave plot, and mine. He had an idea we should mingle our families in death, though why this was important, since we were hardly mingling in life, was unclear.

One clammy, unpromising morning we went on a tour so Hank could take pictures of family plots and get an idea of how he wanted us to be. His family were easy to find. There were so many plots and they each had fancy, fantasy graves. One was dominated by a larger-than-life headless statue of Matthew Willoughby, who had been lost at sea. Another had a row of knee-high pillars of little Willoughbys who had succumbed to the influenza epidemic of 1897. These children had had beautiful names, Ezekiel, Everitas, Eliachim. Their stones looked like stained and broken teeth.

There were some weatherworn stones with my name, Yarmouth, on them, though I didn't recognize any of the first names and didn't look back even when Hank, following me, pointed them out. I could tell he was disappointed that I didn't take an interest. He said that my aunt had bred too much California into me.

At one site, Hank had me hold his camera. He crouched beside a mossy unmarked grave with serpentine edges, putting the side of his face to it, as if he were listening. I looked at him, his bulk exaggerated in that bent-over position, the fog hanging round him, cheek to cheek with a tombstone, trying to hear something. The stone and the man made an oddly erotic and domestic pair in the earthlight of the graveyard, and I thought to myself, This is where his heart is, I've located it. This is what he is tied to, these are his connections. I felt nothing at all. It was unnerving.

Eliza wanted to take pictures too, and Hank gave her the camera. She photographed small flat squares in the earth that had single initials on them, *P* or *M,* and also stones that had decorations in front of them, a flag, a wreath, a heart made out of carnations with "Mom" written in flowers. I stood watching her and she told me my foot was in a lot of the pictures.

Going back in the car, Hank told Eliza stories about his family, her family. He wanted her to know about her heritage, he said. And it was a long story, going a long way back before it hit glory, when the Willoughbys owned timberlands and mills, and they were the most important people in town. Hank's grandfather had attended the school his great-grandfather built, but his own father didn't have time for school because he had to earn money after fires destroyed the business. Then he told her about how much his own father had loved his mother (Eliza's grandmother) and his mother's mother and how he took care of them; no matter how bleak times were, Hank's father always had a cheerful word for his wife, and a kiss. He reached over and put his hand on my leg, but he addressed the back seat. "That's my family, Eliza. And our family. I love family life."

"I hate family life," she boomed from the back of the station wagon. Hank nearly lost the wheel. The car came to a full stop. I noticed a wildness in Hank's eyes. But he started the car again.

"Just kidding," Eliza said.

"You're a good joker, E," Hank said. His lips made motions of a smile and stayed in it. The sun broke through then. We were driving down a road near home that is dense with trees on either side, trees that cast shadows onto the road. When the sun comes through the branches, it's like being inside a kaleidoscope, and for a short time we were caught up in the jumble of the leaves and the light. Hank pointed out that the weather was just right to do some planting. I suddenly remembered we were out of milk.

My reticence was a signal to Eliza to jump out almost before the car stopped and run for the hoe. "Go get your milk," Hank said, patting my head before he slammed the door. I moved over to the driver's seat and drove down to the store and got the milk and a few good-looking tomatoes and drove home.

Eliza was already watering her geranium, a white one she had planted near the garage, which meant Hank had already dug the hole for her and set up the hose and gotten all his own tools out, and the fertilizer.

He had a love for land—land, earth, and dirt—that I had never managed to work up. My idea of beautiful ground is probably a composition court. Yet in Whitby Cove, where of all places I should really feel at home, where my own mom had lived and thought about that man who gave me to her and then walked out of her life, where my body first took shape, I felt enclosed, restricted, wound up in Hank's dreams of his phlox and his willow trees. He seemed to take up all the room there was. Whereas I had one name for things here, he had a string of them, including nicknames, Latin names, provincial-variety names. I really think he could name every growing thing in Latin without once having to consult his books.

He put his hand on my shoulder. He sniffed at my neck. "What is that?" he said.

"Ambush," I said.

"I didn't give that to you."

"I know. It's cologne from the pharmacy. I made up the name. I don't know what it's called."

"It's wrong for you. You need something lighter, more floral." Then, "Can we make love tonight?" he said.

"Okay."

"Can you try to show a little spirit, Kate?"

"I'll try. Where's Eliza?"

"She's by the river. I told her it was all right. Where are you going?"

"In the house. I want to get out of this skirt."

"Don't change."

"What?"

"Please keep your skirt on. You look right in it."

"I don't feel right in it. Anyway, why is it such a big deal for you. You're so weird about me and my clothes."

"Because I'm right. It's the way you should look. Believe me, I know what I'm talking about. Indulge me on this."

"Why?"

"Because it's important to me."

"That's what I'm asking you. Why is it important to you?"

"You should stay covered up. You're too brown. Your skin can't take it."

"I use a sunscreen. You gave it to me. Besides, my skin has always been dark."

"Couldn't have been. Couldn't have been dark when you were a baby."

"Baby Kate is twenty-nine years old now. You met her only a few years ago. She was twenty-two then."

"Please just don't change. I also like it when you wear that straw hat."

"It's four o'clock in the afternoon, Hank, and it is probably going to rain." There was a cauldron of clouds forming across the river. They were all of a piece and traveling fast. I had a feeling it was important to stay in this conversation, but I was having trouble keeping up any momentum at all. I said, "I'm not changing my skirt and I am not putting on my hat. How's that?"

"Okay," he said. "No hat. But I bet Alice would like you to wear your hat."

"I don't like it when you call my mother Alice." He always did that when he wanted to tease me, acted as if he knew her. At first it had surprised me when he remembered her name and used it. But by now it irritated me.

It occurred to me that I shouldn't have been so agreeably compromising, and it also occurred to me that it was pointless not to be, on such incidentals. My aunt Kate came into my head, my aunt and another one of her frog stories, this one about the frog that jumped into the spaghetti pot. The pot was on the stove and there was a light under it. But the water was cold and the frog swam lazily in it. At one point it occurred to the frog that the water was getting warm and it might be a good idea to jump out. But jumping out would have required a great effort. It was easier to stop thinking and relax in the water. He was after all just getting a little uncomfortable. Soon after that the frog passed out and got cooked with the spaghetti.

I said, "Do you think it's safe for Eliza by herself down there?"

"Kate, will you let that child off the leash?"

"Right," I said, heading down toward the river. I wasn't afraid for her. I just wanted to be with her.

Eliza was off somewhere else, so I just sat on the bank and looked out over the marshes, which, at that weak time of day, looked like flat wilderness. The noise in my head was uncomfortable, an aerial surf that found confirmation in the rending clouds ahead of me and in the dampness that crept into my feet and the growing conviction that I was living out the length of a life all right but that I was farther and farther from base. Though I could not say what that base was.

I thought about Eliza in the old days, arching away

from me and saying her first word, "Hi," which she said repeatedly until I thought I would begin to howl. Then I saw her a little farther downstream, crouched in the sand-bottomed shallows among the wet rocks. She was popping seaweed.

I went back and forth a lot from the country to the city because I didn't have one long vacation, as Hank did, which I liked. I liked the physical distance and I liked my summer work project. I was putting together a glossary of risk-management products. My job was to go around and interview the people who thought these things up. The risk instruments had names that sounded like sports talk: knock-in option, fraption, floortion, delta hedging, droplock swap, butterfly spread, straddle, strangle, puttable swap. It made for interesting days, and it would have been the perfect time to have an affair, to bring a little life into me so I could give it back to Hank. I knew these things could work, even if they were false relations. And couldn't I have an affair if I wanted to? Was I so ugly?

Then, all of a sudden, I had a chance. An old boy-friend sent me an invitation. He said he was coming through on his way to play the circuit in Europe, and did I want to get together? He enclosed a worn and well-folded paper on which he had put one of those self-sticking notes, asking: "Remember this?" It was a letter

I had written him the first week I was in graduate school. I recognized my handwriting but I hardly recognized the person I was when I sent it:

Want to play tennis, Doug? You won't be sorry. Out here in the truly big-time East, I hit a hard backhand and I run like all get-out. I am much faster now, you wouldn't believe it. I remember you said once when I came back from the courts and you were waiting for me in my bed that it was one of the best waits you ever had. You were reading Isaac Asimov on Curiosity which I had been reading to you before I had to go play doubles. I would like to go visit you in your bed now, after my game, when I'm oh so much better than I was before. You would stand back and whistle if you saw me running across the court these days, racket up because I'm just going to flick the ball close to the net on your side, or maybe I'm going to hit a low one crosscourt again, or a deep one, straight on, and I'm running up with my racket ready and my legs moving so fast and I'm just about to get that ball and then I flip over onto you and you're so surprised but you catch me and hold me for a moment away from you but secure in your grip, such great forearms, such control, and then you ease me down toward you and I'm maybe a little sweaty but not much because this is fall and the oak leaves are even on the court sometimes, they make a quiet crackling sound like nothing else in the world, the outdoors at its absolute best, and I'm coming closer to you now, I'm in there, in your arms, crossing over your heart.

My hand got so clammy reading my own words that the old paper stuck to my hand and I had to peel it off and hold it away from me to throw it away. No, I wasn't interested in seeing Doug. I wasn't interested in anything, it seemed, or I was scared or I was embarrassed or I had changed or I was no longer curious or I didn't want to fix my marriage.

In any case, I had given up on the marriage, except to feel bad about it. It was the price I paid for not loving Hank. I thought it was a fair price.

That summer it seemed that Jack Cardiff, my ex-neighbor who lived across the park now, and I were the only ones in New York. I gathered Jack was someone out of a job on Wall Street, where he had made some money. He was now married to a wealthy woman, for whom he scouted investments involving companies that had discovered a new way to extract oil from the ground, or cauterize wounds, or melt steel. We kept meeting each other in the park; he would be between tennis dates or between appointments. We got in the habit of taking walks together, which was tedious for me because he was such a slow walker. But he always seemed to know when I was going out, and he'd show up suddenly nearby. So I could hardly avoid him.

There was nothing very personal in our talking and walking. He did say, setting a tone that stayed with me, that he had thought that by this time in his life he would have a number of very good friends, and that he didn't have a number of these good friends. We were on a knoll near my house by then, and I had to go in. From that time I took away the impression that life had not treated him properly. It made me want to do something nice for him.

And that was a good feeling for me, one I hadn't had in a while.

In July, at the country club beach party, Eliza won the blue ribbon in the crab-walk contest and second prize in the foot race. That summer she also swam in deep water for the first time and learned to ride a two-wheeler bike. The bike was a goal she set for herself. She said she didn't want to go back without having learned because Benjamin could ride his bike.

As far as I knew, Eliza had one moral dilemma. We had visitors who brought a little dog with them. We were all invited to a birthday dinner up the road in a house with cats. So we left the little dog tied up outside our house. When we got up to the party, we discovered we had forgotten the birthday present, and so Eliza went down to get it. She was gone a long time and when she came back, she looked very sad. She told me this: "I went down for the present and the dog was crying and I talked to him and then I tried to leave and he started

crying again, and then I knew that if I left him he'd still
be crying and then he peed on my dress and I went in to
wash it and I cried and I thought, I have to leave him
because I have to bring up the present. So I left him. But
I don't think it's right."

I made her a sandwich and sent her back to the
puppy.

On the whole, there were no dramatic victories because
there was no struggle. There was a sense of hanging on
and waiting. When Hank and I were alone in each
other's company, we were together in a thickening
gloom. It began to feel as if it had always been this way,
that it could never be any other way, that life was indeed
a dead-gray road and we were traveling it in a cart that
got stuck in all the ruts. We seemed to have lost the will
to strive, and as a consequence, we could wind up lin-
gering indefinitely in a complacency marked by fainter
and fewer sensations. Meanwhile we were developing a
quiet deference toward each other, beyond which we
didn't want to or could not go. We respected each
other's wishes and tastes. We lived in reciprocal indiffer-
ence to the other's world, a situation that in itself was
growing dull. Even the fact that I did not regret what we
had become together stopped worrying me.

And what had we become together? Certainly risk-
averse. Most people are risk-averse, Hank used to say,

implying he was not. Most people are too scared to apply the first rule of successful speculating to their own lives. That rule is: Cut your losses short, take them early. Most people have trouble taking small losses. As a result, small losses turn into moderate losses, which are even harder to take. Finally the moderate losses turn into big losses, which you are forced to take. All because it was too hard to take the first small loss as soon as it showed up.

But were we now at the point of no return? This big loss that we were going to be forced to take, would it be more destructive if we withdrew now or more destructive if we did not withdraw now?

Eliza was watchful. She developed a routine of setting the table for Hank and me after her own dinner. She would put us very close together in a corner. She insisted on candlelight. She made a parade of very small animals on the table and talked to them, and to us, while we ate. She made a list of what she wanted to plant in her garden: daylilies, lilacs, burning bush. She always stayed through dinner.

Late one August afternoon, about a week before we were supposed to go back to the city, Eliza said she wanted to leave that very day because she missed her friend Benjamin too much. I said I wasn't sure he would be there, because the family wasn't coming back until fall. Eliza cried hard. Then she got out some paper and said, "I'm writing him a letter right now." And she did. The letter said: "Dear Benjamin, I miss you so much that if I don't see you soon, I'll wish I never lived. I wish I had you again. I miss you. Lots of love, Eliza."

We drove down to the post office to mail the letter and on the way back I got her an ice-cream cone. The evening was settling in. There was a feeling of oppression, as if the flatness that seemed to overtake us both when we paused outside the store were in actuality the leaden sky coming down on us. We stood looking across the low line of river and the dark marshes beyond. Eliza said, "You're wrong, Mom. It's fall already. Look how many leaves have fallen in the dark."

"A lot of leaves," I agreed.

Benjamin's mother died the second Wednesday in September. The housekeeper gave me the story.

Pain had woken up Isabel at four in the morning on her last day, and she asked Chuck to take her to the hospice, as she had planned. As soon as she was tucked into her hospice bed, she began to sink. Her brothers were with her, and her husband and Benjamin and the housekeeper. Isabel passed into unconsciousness and stopped breathing. The hospice workers did not try to revive her. Isabel's color began to change. Her face relaxed and she was gone. The hospice workers could not have been kinder. They said to the family, Don't worry, you don't have to leave. They said, Let's take off her rings now. They said, Let's put a towel under her chin.

The school telephoned the class parent representative, who called the weather-alert mothers—I was one of those—and we each phoned our group of mothers in the class so that they would be prepared when their children came home. Benjamin had told the children on the playground. He said his mother had a tumor of the neck and it grew until her neck exploded. I called my group and left messages about Isabel Dover's death but I didn't talk about how Benjamin delivered the news.

When Eliza got off the bus, the sun was golden on her and she jumped into my arms. She had an envelope for me.

"Open it fast. Philip says it's a love letter." (Philip was the bus driver.) She opened it for me. It was the bill for the school bus. "Very interesting," Eliza said. "Here." She pulled a paper plane out of her pocket and straightened it out. "This is for you too." Little arrows pointed to little signs that said "Open here." I opened. It read, "Hello, dodo brain."

She wanted cocoa, so I made cocoa. "How was school today?"

"Okay. We had math again. I hate math."

"Anything happen?"

"No."

"I heard that Benjamin's mother died. That's sad."
No response.

"Where is your headband?" I said.

Silence.

"I'm going to a meeting of the parents tonight at your school."

"What for?"

The force of her dark eyes gave me pause, but I said, "To talk about how everybody feels about Benjamin's mother's dying," I said.

"I don't think Benjamin wants everybody saying things about his mother. I'm sure he wouldn't like it. I don't think you should go." I made a move to pick her up and hold her but she ducked me.

The meeting was in the cafeteria. Tea was set up. The china cups were cold against the lips. A psychiatrist spoke. He was exceptionally boring. He said, "There are some real cognitive questions here. How can you die and not be part of the world?" Then the mothers started up and it got much more interesting. One child had told his mother that Benjamin said his mother wanted to be burnt to ashes, and the child wanted to know what it felt like to be burnt to ashes. Another mother said her daughter was afraid of Benjamin. Another child had told her mother that Benjamin wasn't sad because now he would get all his mother's things and he could sell them and make money.

The final word from the psychiatrist was that we should follow our child's lead. "If your child can put off the pain of what is going on, let him. He needs to be protected too. A child's feelings are a mystery to him, and he may be afraid his parents won't accept his feelings."

When I got home, Eliza was in bed listening to a fairy tale tape. "Where have you been?" she said. I reminded her about the meeting at her school. "Were all the parents there?"

"I think so," I said.

"Why did they have to go?"

"Well, everyone has feelings about Benjamin's mother and we all want to talk about our feelings. Don't you want to talk about it?"

"I wanted to ask Benjamin how he knew his mother was dead, but I don't think he wanted to tell me."

"Why don't you ask him if he wants to talk about it?"

"I don't think he wants me to ask him. Would you turn over my tape, please?"

"How was school today?"

"Some of it was good and some of it was bad."

"Tell me one good part."

"I'm tired, Mom."

That night Eliza appeared suddenly in my room, screaming. She stood about two feet from the bed, straight up, in her nightgown with the lace collar and lavender bow, hair in a curly mass, so that her head seemed much too big for her slip of a body. She was like a watchdog, sharp and intense, blacking apart the dark with her cones of barking. She kept restarting. The screams were short, loud, repetitive, and all the same length, like the Count on *Sesame Street,* when he says *ah, ah, ah, ah, ah.*

When I picked her up, she was stiff and light as an unopened envelope. I carried her back to her bed and laid her down. I got in with her under her comforter. She stopped her noise immediately and fell asleep.

It was a fitful night, cramped and dark there with Eliza snoring beside me. I kept sensing that I was toppling over. It was a very old feeling, a regular night feeling I used to get in my aunt's bed, when something scared me enough to make me brave a trip to her room, where my uncle almost never was but she always was, and usually with her, I remember, the voice of Arthur Godfrey coming from the radio on her night table. It made me wonder all over again how could there be so much stirring in a room with only my aunt and a radio and me. That radio seemed to find its way into her pillows even, so that I almost couldn't tell whether it was him or her croaking at me to stop whining. I always had to plead, but I always did plead, and she always took me in. And I would lie in the dark on my side of the pillows, listening to her breathing—so heavy the way she let out air after she'd rumpled up Kleenex all over her side and under her head pillow and on the bed stand, where the radio played that voice till her breathing drowned it out. She was so loud next to me. Maybe she just seemed loud. I could afford that thought because I was safe beside her. I could afford to think she was pretty disgusting and I could afford not to care if I rolled over on her Kleenex box because I wasn't afraid anymore.

I thought of Isabel, her red lips and her bald head. I thought of her breathing in the hospice, her breath floating on the bedsheets.

The next morning I asked Eliza, "What were you dreaming last night?" and I told her about her screaming. She hung her head and a tear dropped straight down on the linoleum floor and she said, "Why are you trying to scare me? I had no dreams. I didn't come into your room."

Then, "What am I doing after school today?" She moved to find her date book, her very complete date book. She discovered that Andrew was coming home with her. "I don't want Andrew to come here." Eliza started to cry again. The color under her eyes deepened.

"Why not?" I reached for her. She was too quick.

"He said I didn't really hurt my ankle when I hurt my ankle."

"When did you hurt your ankle?"

"Yesterday. When Benjamin hurt his. We both have sprained ankles. Andrew said I was faking. I don't like him."

It was too late to do anything about this, and difficult anyway because she was whimpering loudly and it was hard to think through the whimpering. I said, "You feel very close to Benjamin." And she said, "Our feelings are connected." And I said, "Maybe that's why your ankle hurt." And she said, "No, I really hurt my ankle and Andrew didn't believe me." She started crying again and she went to school crying.

And I thought to myself, Does she know this marriage is dead? Am I giving out any clues?

I had a walk date with Jack Cardiff that day, but it was raining. He suggested we have lunch around the corner. I told him sure, but I'd be late, because I had telephoning to do, so he should go ahead without me and I'd come when I could.

He was already there when I arrived, looking exactly the same as he always looked, neat and polite, wearing exactly the same clothes he always wore, with the same dark soft scarf draped down over his muted herringbone jacket. He was eating vegetables and brown rice and drinking herbal tea. Weak herbal tea. We talked about a project of his in which he seemed to have little interest—something about starting a credit-card operation in Manila, I think. All the time he was looking near me but not at me.

It struck me as dreary and sad—his punctuality, his inability to talk straight across a table, his fastidious, beautiful dress. I had planned to ask him about his current marriage, but that seemed like such an intrusion, so unfair, when he was so clearly unhappy and confused about life. Probably even at that moment he was asking himself, How did I end up in this dreary sad place on the West Side in the rain with a woman who insults me by coming late? The vegetables were steamed and had no dressing whatsoever on them. There was an awful lot of cabbage on his plate. I thought he was too old to be eating this way; there didn't seem any need to be so ascetic in the last third of his life, but I kept quiet about it.

I was bored, and I had just arrived. Civilized behavior dictated I stay at least forty-five minutes. I felt safe in my own neighborhood. I decided to take a conversational risk.

I said, "My husband tracks my periods."

My voice was clear. "He marks a circle with a dot in the middle on his pocket calendar. The morning after we make love, he marks an *x* on the date. He stands at his bureau in his undershorts and opens his pocket calendar to the week we're in and picks up a pen. He puts the pen between his teeth and pulls it with his other hand to release the writing end. He keeps the top in his mouth while he marks the *x*. Then he fits the pen back together and takes it out of his mouth and closes the pocket calendar and finishes dressing."

"Your husband," he said. His fork was in the air.

"It's about sovereignty," I said.

His fork was still in the air. His big scarf swam before my eyes. My head began to hurt.

"It's about divorce," I said. "I am going to get a divorce."

"I know," he said.

"How did you know?"

"I can spot these things."

His scarf fell in wide drifts down onto his jacket. I couldn't see the fringe.

"I can help you," he said. "I have experience."

"Yes, but you never talk about it."

"I'm very good with women who are getting unmarried. I know all about how to go about it."

"Good with women who are getting unmarried?"

And there followed a list: He had first guided his mother and then his aunt and then his younger aunt and then planned his own divorce, and then, when he had married again and made sure all his children were still with him, he had started befriending women who were leaving their husbands, the wives of his tennis partners, several journalists, a jeweler. There were more.

"Why do you want to tell me this?"

"Because I want you to know you aren't alone."

"Being part of a list can make you feel alone."

"I'm sorry. I didn't mean it like that."

"How did you mean it?"

"I meant, I am here for you. Talk to me. Use me."

The rain stopped and we went outside. On the way through the park, on the sidewalk, I saw colors I didn't expect in among the oak leaves and the chestnuts and acorns: bright scraps that must have come from umbrellas, because they had snaps on them, and a bunch of fresh petals that had to have been torn from the flowers, because they were still fresh and rosy, and huge with colors of the body's private insides. I could see us, too, without colors, in the puddles, our whole bodies reflected in the shallowest puddle, and even trees, entire trees, several lifetimes of growth in a single shallow puddle, and the clouds moving through the bare branches of the trees, again reflected. I saw the clouds by looking down into the puddle. It seemed incredible to me, my life opening up, expanding in a puddle, all there was up to then perfectly clear. There must be an explanation for that—it's definitely a science question, how an entire landscape and the people in it can be so fully revealed in a puddle.

There was something about Jack's voice. It was a cool but serious voice. Such a thumping sound. I wanted to put my hands on it, to press against the loose scarf on his neck, take the scarf and go home with it, maybe bring him, too. His kettledrum voice and the scarf.

"If you have only two wishes, what's the second wish?" He said. He had both his hands in his jacket pockets.

"I give up."

"Two more wishes." He freed one hand and cut a spiral in the air, raising his arm higher and higher.

This was a dream I had that night.

Jack is in a corner of the living room. He is seated on a sofa next to the piano, his smooth, clean hands holding on to each other, the sofa cushions puffed up around his legs. He crosses his legs when he sees me. His hair is dyed the flyaway orange of school safety-patrol cloaks. His eyes are wet, his face composed. The day before he had run through the halls of his house in Menlo Park, chasing after the nurse who takes care of him, though it offends him to say so. He would rather the nurse acknowledge his romantic plans for the two of them. Now he holds his fingers that were squeezed in the doorjamb. Part of his hand is still exposed, and I can see the scars left by the fork that he plunged through his thumb joint during a previous encounter with the nurse, whom he loves "beyond all telling." I ask him to play. He demurs. He plays. His own composition. It sounds like leaves swirling to the ground on a windy day. A sunny but windy day. He plays the same bits over and over again, so distinctly repetitive that I am quickly aware of the circles of his ceaseless frenzy. After about ten minutes, interrupting himself in mid-redundant-phrase, he stands and shuts down the keyboard lid, explaining, "I can't remember any more."

Hank and I went back to Whitby Cove that fall weekend, taking Benjamin with us. The children were beginning to have some trouble coming to a meeting of minds. Benjamin asked Eliza which she liked best—Dodge, Lincoln, or Chrysler?

"What are you talking about?" she said.

He tried again. They saw the sign for the George Washington Bridge and Benjamin said, "When do you actually reach New Jersey?"

Hank said, "When you cross the George Washington Bridge."

"When you are halfway across it?" Benjamin pressed. But Hank was cut off by Eliza.

"George Washington was a good president," she

said. She felt she had the floor, so she added, "I'm not for Bush. He wants to take away from the poor and give to the rich."

And Benjamin said, "I don't mind Barbara Bush so much."

"Let's not talk about this anymore," Eliza said.

"We shouldn't have started talking about the George Washington Bridge," said Benjamin.

We stopped after a while at McDonald's and the children got Happy Meals with toucan-beak disguises in them.

The marsh grass on the Apachanack River was light and brushy. The trees on the other side of the river were turning brown, red, and yellow. The yellow was a soft mustard color but the red was scarlet and sharp.

The first night we roasted marshmallows over the fire and carved pumpkins and put candles in them. While they were working on the pumpkins, Eliza told Benjamin a story. She said it was going to be a Halloween story about tombstones and skeletons. She began: "Once there was a little girl who had a sick mother. She died, but before she died she told me that I could take all the stuff that she had that I have wanted so much."

"Is this about your mother?" Benjamin asked.

"No, it's a story."

"Is it about my mother?"

"Nobody's mother. Do you want to hear my story?"

"Okay."

"Okay. I'm telling the story again. I decorated the ground with as many pretty flowers as I could find."

"What ground?" said Benjamin.

"The ground where she was."

"You mean her grave."

"Okay. Should I keep telling my story?"

"Is it long?"

"No. I'm decorating the ground now. Remember? That way the mother said she would protect me. I was coming out the door one day, when I banged my finger in the door, but it didn't even hurt because I was near the place where the mother was in the ground.

"One day I went to a store and I bought some tiger lilies and I took them to the ground where she was, and every day I came to smell them.

"Sometimes I'm in my sleeping bag and I sleep on top of her. She is under the dirt and I am on top of the dirt. I asked the person who made my sleeping bag to make the word *Mother* all over it and the exact picture of the . . . what is that word, Benjamin?"

"What word? *Grave*," said Benjamin.

"Good. Exact picture of the grave."

Benjamin hadn't moved, so Eliza kept going. "One day I went to the same store and bought some new baby's-breath and a dead butterfly to go along with it. Whenever I see my mother's grave, I always like to sit there and eat lunch, and once in a while I get up and I hug it and I cover it with lipstick kisses. I sent so much love into that ground that it came to Mother and stirred up her heart. She wasn't dead in the first place. She was just ice-cold.

"Did you like that story, Benjamin?"

Benjamin asked if they could listen to the Beatles tape and Eliza put it on.

The children took the pumpkins up to bed with them, and before we turned the lights out, we blew their candles out. They slept peacefully all night.

From my bed, very early, I heard an argument.

"Benjamin, you idiot! You made me fall in the cereal."

"I'm sorry. I hate Variety Pak."

"Why?"

"Because there's only one Frosted Flakes. I wish I had never come."

"Why?"

"Because then we wouldn't have to fight about the Frosted Flakes."

"It's okay. I'm having Rice Krispies anyway. Except you messed them all up. Please don't be sorry you came."

"I can't wait until we get married," he said.

"Why?" she said.

"So we can get a divorce," he said.

It was quiet then for a while. They went outside and came back with a basket full of twigs and dirt clumps and some flowers. Eliza really liked using the fancy flower-cutting scissors Hank had ordered. "Mom," Eliza said to me as I opened the screen door for them, "why didn't you call me Force Flower or Isabel?"

Benjamin put the twigs near the fire and took out the Clue game. He likes the weapons. He got some pens and paper and started copying them and writing the names down underneath his drawings.

Eliza was in the kitchen, putting the flowers into cups. She called to him: "Benjamin, come here. I need some help with these cups."

No answer.

"Benjamin?"

"I'm busy. I'm drawing. Okay?"

No answer. Eliza came out of the kitchen, carrying a mug of flowers. "These are for us, Benjamin. How do you like them?"

No answer. Eliza clomped up the stairs. She had flowers for every room, and when she finished placing them, she and Benjamin lined up some marshmallows for toasting. Hank came in and wanted to know what the marshmallows were doing on the chair.

"They're just lying there," Benjamin said.

"What are they thinking?" Eliza joined in.

"They're not thinking," Benjamin answered.

"How do they feel?" Eliza kept up.

"They don't feel anything. That's what it means to be dead." He picked up one and toasted it. Eliza did the same.

"Benjamin, what's the difference between heaven and hell?" Eliza asked.

"Hell's bad and heaven's great," said Benjamin, sticking his stick through two marshmallows and putting the stick to the fire.

Then we went down to the beach. It was a windy day. Benjamin traced a line, maybe sixty feet long. Eliza drew hearts. She put an arrow with many feathers through the heart, dividing it in two. On the top she wrote "Mom" and on the bottom she wrote "Dad." Benjamin all the while was hunched over his line, deepening it. A sliver of his bare back showed but he took no notice.

Back home, Eliza and Benjamin bailed out the motorboat in the river. They worked in tandem, trading off a jug and a water pump. I watched them pouring water into the river.

A short time later, the children were in the house playing a game that consisted in giving Hank and me little tests. If we passed we would win prizes. I got a prize for figuring out two times three. The prize was a tiny address book. "Here's your prize. Be sure to write your husband's address in there," said Eliza.

Hank went outside to put his tools away for the

winter. I took some baskets out, to store them in the garage but mostly to watch Hank. I liked to see him when he handled his tools.

I remembered his getting the ground ready once in the early days. He was using a pickax and stones were flying and I went around in front of him and knelt down near him, next to a hole he had already finished the main digging for. We were going to plant two cedar trees. I rubbed my arms with dirt the way he always did to get the feel of it, then plunged in with a short spade.

Hank reached over and took away my spade. "Not that. That's for geraniums. You see why? It has a very deep curve, you see, it cups my hand. It's for bulb beds, so you can dig the right depth but not the ground around the hole.

"Take these," he said, and gave me a three-pronged fork and a wide spade. I pulled back. The tools were so shiny that even though the sun wasn't bright they hurt my eyes. He noticed. "I ordered these specially," he said. "They're stainless steel. No rust. Dirt doesn't stick to them, so you get less friction when you dig. Makes it easier." I took the tools from him, one in each hand. The handles were warm. "Those are going to last longer than we will," he said, and was suddenly silent. I looked at him as he flushed in his enthusiasm, in his earnest, bright way. I was for that moment glad to be instructed by him, thinking we had never worked so well together as then, digging those holes.

We left for the city late in the afternoon. Hank drove. I pushed the seat back and the sun hit my face. It was warm. I eased into sleep. I dreamed I was given a gift. It was a soft, squishy fur-covered doll. I buried my head in its head. The doll's face began to disappear and the white fur around the blankening face began to darken, to take on a smutty tinge, darker and darker.

In the city that night, Eliza woke up about one-thirty. She came into our room. "It's too noisy," she said. I didn't hear anything, but I didn't argue. The floor of her room is white. It glows. "There is not enough light in here," she said. "I need the bathroom light on." I turned on the bathroom light. She pretended to sleep. I pushed off the bed the giant bear with the stuffing all in one side of the head and the big green floor frog and a few others. I was cold. I got in bed with her at her end, under the story of the Little Fur Family, which is written on the comforter, and the next morning, from her bed, we heard the alarm go off in my bedroom.

Eliza's frog must have died that night because I found it the next morning in a corner of the cage. The worms were alive and they were crawling over the frog. Hank was for telling Eliza and having a proper burial in Central Park. But I hid the frog in the laundry room until I could find a replacement. She never knew the difference.

All that week Eliza broke things. She dropped her porcelain yak from Afghanistan and two legs came off. She broke several of her doll teacups. She brought me her rhino, now without any tusks. It looked as if the second tusk had been twisted off. She said, "It fell." She wanted to bring a plaster egg to show-and-tell. I said, "You should wrap that in something soft and put it in a shoe box." She said she could handle it. She dropped the egg in the lobby as she was getting out of the elevator.

She drew a picture of tombstones and gave it to me. She had written on only one of them. She wrote, "Here lies Mom dead. Poor Mom." I told her that it was odd to have my name on a tombstone because I didn't even feel sick.

"No, that's Benjamin's mom."

"Is this from the story you told Benjamin?"

"What story?"

"Never mind," I said.

"What do you think is happening to her?" I asked Hank. We were sitting down to dinner, just the two of us.

"I think you're driving her crazy. But if I have to spend this whole dinner talking about Eliza, I'm going to get the paper."

So we talked about whether or not we should get a Wedgwood-blue rocking chair for the living room. It was the right price in a store on Broadway, and it would be easy to get it home. But was it too tacky for our taste? Were we after elegance? We were after elegance. On the other hand, the color was good. It would fit in well.

And so the dinner hour passed and we put the dishes in the dishwasher and turned on the dishwasher and turned out the lights and went to bed.

The next day was Eliza's annual checkup and I went early to school to pick her up. Her class was in the gym, moving to music. They were just about to do the favorite, the night scene, in which the moon rises and the animals come out looking for food. The music started playing, Chopin, I think, and Mrs. Driscoll began her narration: "It was a dark and stormy night. And then the clouds blew away and the moon started to rise, ray by ray." The girls who were the moon stood up one by one and joined hands in a circle and walked around. Then Eliza and the other children came out. They were foxes and skunks and bears and weasels and possums, who hung on the bar by one leg. One by one the animals went to sleep and "the moon pulled back in the sky, ray by ray."

As Mrs. Driscoll was talking, Benjamin pulled a chair from a corner of the room to the center and stood on it and put his arms straight up over his head and turned around on the chair. So all the children were lying asleep on the floor and Benjamin was standing on his chair with his arms reaching above his head and he was grave and solemn when he turned, slowly, slowly, slowly, turning.

Then all the children pretended they were horses from the carousel let loose at night, but as on a carousel, they stayed together in a pack, holding hands, and they ran around the room in a deafening stampede. Except for Benjamin, who pranced, and shook his head so that his hair fell round him like a mane, and whinnied. In all that noise, you could hear him whinnying. And then he broke free, and he was suddenly alone among all the children, a horse in the night, let loose in the park and way out ahead, free to move forward with the music. I saw him so free, without death, the death over and gone, gone over the hill, where he might go someday, surely he would go, but what matter, not this night in the moonlight. Now he was free of his carousel and loping forward. I remembered something the psychiatrist had promised that night we were all together in the cafeteria. "Benjamin will not be a reminder of death for long" was what he had said.

Part II

Intro

There was a family memorial service for Isabel Dover right before Christmas. The school did not take part. I knew about it because Benjamin couldn't spend the night because of it. I decided to attend on my own. I was emotionally related to Isabel, I told Hank when he asked me if it wasn't just for family. He didn't argue, only asked me to be home by noon as he had a lunch to go to. The bank was involved in a deal with the Tokyo Financial Futures Exchange and he had meetings for almost every meal.

It was a stony, raw day. A chill permeated the church and seemed to bore most acutely into the left chapel, where the service was. I was late and cold and unhappy and in the back, and it all seemed a rumbly mumble in the hard, still air, and it was difficult to concentrate on the matter at hand.

I tried thinking generally about things, hoping to home in on the minister and make some sort of connection. What I came up with was that we save the small words for the big things. For example, God.

About God, if God, Jung said: Proofs don't do any good. We might as well be Australian wool-eating moths trying to prove to other moths that Australia exists.

I don't know about Australia, but I can work up to believing in certain things. Like uncertainty, opposites, the life of stones, the rearrangement of molecules, even in stones. I agree that the unseen overwhelms the seen and that the unexpected belongs in this world. The unexpected is what makes life whole. (Jung again.)

I believe in connections, connections that go from the seen to the unseen and back, from the unknown to the known and back. And forth. And up and down. And among generations and across bloodlines. Connections not necessarily between two people. Because people are not the same, moment to moment. Solid flesh, mine, Isabel's, Eliza's, is illusion. We are at all times engulfed by decay and regeneration. We are transients, and yet the body remembers. Somehow it hangs on to its connections. A single glance, a disembodied voice, can call up a pattern of hopes and desires.

Maybe it's about patterns. We are not the same person we were a year ago but we are of the same pattern. Physically, anyway. Once we learn how to play catch or ride a bike or speak, we never forget. And a person's signature looks the same year to year. It looks the same when it's written big on the blackboard and small on a piece of paper, too, though entirely different sets of muscles are used in each case.

How much of our life is ruled by patterns that have no voice other than their spontaneous articulation in repetition.

The point is that something connects and repeats the patterns. Habit, maybe, or thought, or atoms. Atom to atom, cell to cell, molecule to molecule, less a connection than a thread, a wave, a vibration.

It is a wave, a vibration of memory, perhaps.

The fact of longing, that longing exists, longing itself, is evidence that something else is present, however unformed. The body remembers, and somewhere in it a vigil is kept.

I couldn't make out who was talking—reading, rather—though I could feel the rhythms of Scripture and I could see Isabel in a way. I could at least see her better than I could see God, for example. So I sat in church and willed Isabel to me. I willed her near me, using the commando confidence of my childhood. And I felt her, a silent presence, big as the moon, with the milky immanence proper to moonlight. And with her light came clarity. Peace. Pardon. All that.

A short time after Christmas, our family entered into a silhouette period, as if we were carrying on a shadow play behind a scrim. In our shadow play, ordinary concerns took on a metaphorical, sometimes foreboding character. Eliza ventured deeper into her doll world and discovered chaos and unhappiness. She concocted medicines and ministered incessantly. Hank grew nearly morbid about his plantings, which were being torn apart, he imagined, by the bad winter weather, but he would not take a day off to go see them.

Habit kept us going. Our routines. Our conventions. Hank and I took to doing what people do when they don't want their husbands or wives around anymore. They pretend they are strangers. We became exceedingly polite, one to the other. Polite and remote.

There is something, though not much, to be said for

habit. Habit lulls the spirit. It's bloodless and mindless. It makes life go smoothly. It organizes energy. It's safe. On the other hand, habit disconnects the senses and makes us nearly invisible. Habit makes safety undesirable after a while. Still, it was not altogether bad to be in such a haze. Kind of like a rest period.

On several occasions I had the distinct feeling of not measuring up to an unspecified standard, a feeling that was invariably mixed into and lost in a general tide of shame at not being able to help effect the life I believed we ought to be living. I felt embedded in my own sense of failure, so layered that I was almost impenetrable. News couldn't reach me, including, maybe especially, news about Hank. One missed news opportunity I mention here only to show how completely unaware I was.

The bank promoted Hank. He was appointed head of his department. He telephoned me and I went to join him for an impromptu celebration. He was pleased, and so was everyone else, it seemed. I stood by him, a large shy man in a three-piece suit, as he was congratulated. A cluster of people came up and then twos and threes and a bunch more. But it all seemed to take place a few inches aboveground. For him at least. There was no real exchange going on, no eyes meeting eyes, even very few handshakes. It was as if we were in the field during a baseball practice and the batters were hitting here and there and everywhere but where he was. He was adrift on the open ground of middle age, a big, brainy guy without a sport.

Later, in what I thought was a tender moment, as he was looking at a seed catalog, I asked him, "Do you think men ever forgive women for being the ones who have the babies?"

"What makes you think I want to have a baby?"

"Well, don't men ever want to know what it's like, for example, to feel a little person inside and then see her and feel her, pump to pump outside and on top of you?"

"You're talking California, Kate. You don't actually think that men have to be pregnant to know something about renewal."

"No. No. Not renewal. Time. Is there anything that can give men such a sensual grasp of time. I mean, an unborn baby *is* time. Real time, not just clock time."

"You're boring me," he said.

I persisted. "You know what I mean. The idea that there's a direction of time, that arrow, and there's that other kind of time, cycles, you know circles." I drew a circle in the air. For me; he wasn't watching. "The arrow of time is about exhaustion and the clock running out, and the cycles are about—"

"I'm trying to read, Kate."

"About continuity. Deep time rolling over itself inside you. That's what you learn about when you have a baby. It synchronizes you—to the sun, or something like that. It takes over and blots out the arrow for a while and it's a kind of release and it makes you feel important, too."

"Maybe you should try mowing the lawn. Probably have the same effect. Look, I think I'm being enormously tolerant but you're pushing me."

I still wouldn't give up. "I guess what I'm asking is, are things ever as good for you, I mean for men, as they are in your imagination?"

He did not raise his head from the flower-bulb pictures and I retreated. "Well, it was great to see how much the bank thinks of you. It was really a pleasure," I said.

Silence.

"Imagination works sometimes. It helps," he said.

"What do you imagine?"

"That you are the soil and flower of the earth, that you are mother of us all, that you are your mother, who was before you and who always was, and that I am the only man and I will live forever. Okay?"

"Your talk is worse than mine."

"I don't imagine you, Kate. I used to imagine someone like you but not you."

It turned out that what he used to imagine actually was my mother, Alice, but that was later and I'm getting ahead of myself.

· · ·

At the end of January the Christmas tree was still up. Hank was the first to break out of our playacting.

Snow was falling behind the Christmas wreath hanging in the window in the dining room. The red balls shone in the light of the falling snow. I was staring at the green, mossy wreath, its darkening center, the red ribbon shining below the gleaming red balls. I was staring at the mossy dark circle, and I could feel Hank walking toward me. He sat down opposite me and coughed.

He had a bad cold but he had cooked dinner anyway. The risotto was underdone. He wanted to talk. I didn't want to talk, but I couldn't refuse because he had a cold and he had cooked the dinner and I had slipped and mentioned that the risotto was underdone.

He said, "I want to know if you are planning something."

"Something?"

"An affair."

"No. I'm not planning anything." I directed my eyes to the floor and I started counting the black and white tiles.

"Are you having an affair?"

"No." Pause. "There is no one but you." My voice was level. Impossible to count the tiles. I lose track almost immediately. They are so separate, one from the other. One follows the other as if nothing has happened before. I reached for the salad. It was all gone.

"You're so cold to me, Kate."

"I know. I'm sorry."

"You confuse me. Sometimes you're not cold. Lately you're not cold, for example. You're very warm."

"I hadn't noticed that."

"What?" he said.

"That I'm warm." There was a gray spot on one of the white tiles. Either a spot or a shadow.

"You're so often cold and then you're not cold. Every once in a while you touch me. In bed you touch me, but out of bed, hardly ever. Actually, you touched me to-night."

"Yes." (I had reached across him on the stove to turn the spinach off and our sides had rested against each other.)

"It felt good."

"I didn't intend it."

"Don't be mean, Kate."

"I'm sorry. I don't want to be mean."

"I know you don't. That's why we're having this conversation."

"Because I'm mean?"

"Because I'm preoccupied with you. My head is always filled with you and I'm trying to get work done—"

"You need to be able to work." (I know what it's like to be preoccupied with someone, and I felt so bad for him, but on the other hand, I didn't want to give too many reassurances because that made me feel bad too.)

Hank said, "Just tell me this. Do you feel any love for me?"

Pause on my side. In my head, I was pouring Spic and Span into a bucket.

"Tell me what you feel about me," he went on.

"I don't have feelings. I have reactions. You'll have to gauge my feelings by what I do."

"Everyone has feelings."

"I don't feel anything. I am trying to be a nice and caring person and I don't feel anything. I am a blank." Now I was running water into the bucket. Foam and suds.

"You're not blank about Eliza."

"Hank," I said, waking myself up. He moved toward me when I said his name. I looked at the buttonhole of his flannel shirt and I said his name again and then I said, "You'll torture yourself if you put both you and Eliza on the same scale of my affections. What happens between parents and children is something so different, so separate. I know you know this."

"I don't know that." Then, "I know that." He was quiet.

"Would you give me that shirt when you take it off. The buttonhole is unraveling."

He said, "I want you to make a commitment to our marriage."

I had finished everything on my plate and I was so hungry. I said, "My commitment is in my actions." Then I said, "I feel like I haven't eaten anything."

He said, "You can't have a marriage a day at a time. You have to plan it."

I reached for an orange. I said, "I am trying to plan. But you always get so mad if I ask you about any of your projects."

"You used to like making love. Now you don't. It humiliates me. I'm always the supplicant."

"What's 'supplicant' mean?" It was Eliza. Her voice was faint but it had the force of an ocean. She was directly behind her father. God, I thought, all this time we've been living here and I never noticed we don't have enough doors. There's no door between the dining room and the hall, no door between the sitting room and the living room, no door between the dining room and the kitchen, from where Eliza must just have emerged while my head was in my orange.

"Where are your shoes?"

"I'm in the house, Mom."

"You'll catch cold."

"Sup-pli-cant," she said again.

"Someone praying," Hank said.

"Oh," she said. Then: "I want to show you a magic trick."

"Eliza, put your slippers on, please," I said.

"After this." She pulled out her hands to show that she held a fork and a spoon. She banged the spoon on the fork. Then she stuck the fork in her mouth. "Hear it?" she said.

"Hear what?" Hank and I said this together.

"My teeth are an echo. Listen. I'll do it again." She banged the spoon on the fork. She put the fork in her mouth. "Did you hear it?"

"No," I said.

"Yes," Hank said.

"Hear what?" I said.

"You have to *listen,* Mom." Eliza was shaking her head at me.

"I don't get it."

"I'll do it for you again."

"What does it mean, anyway?" I said.

Eliza pulled a slim paperback from her running pants. She showed it to me. It said, in red, *Magic Science Tricks.* She had a Garfield bookmark in the page that was titled "Teeth That Hear." "Read this," she said.

"You read it to me."

"You read it, Dad," she said.

"Okay," he said. " 'Why it works. When you strike the fork you make it vibrate so quickly that it makes a sound. Air carries this sound to your ears and you hear it. Solids like teeth and bones conduct sound better than air. When you put the vibrating fork against your solid teeth, you can hear the soft sound. Hearing aids, worn by some people who are hard-of-hearing, use the bones behind the ears to conduct sound.' "

"Maybe you need a hearing aid," Eliza said, waiting for my answer.

"Maybe," I said. "Good trick, Eliza. Your dad and I are having a discussion now."

"I know," she said.

"Is that why you came in?"

"I wanted to show you my trick. And I didn't have dessert yet."

"What do you want for dessert?"

"What do we have?"

"I don't know. Look in the icebox."

Hank was clearing the table. He and Eliza both went into the kitchen. I saw her hug him and he hugged her back. He seemed not to want to let her go. She was still.

She saw me looking at them.

"Mom, what's your favorite color?"

"Ummmmmm."

"Blue," Hank said. He was looking into Eliza's eyes.

"I thought so," she said.

"Why did you think so?" Hank said. He was smoothing her hair.

"Because everything in this house is blue."

"Ask your daddy what his favorite color is," I said.

"Blue," he said.

"That's why everything is blue?"

"You got it, babychuck," I said.

They both turned round and faced me. "That's not the way you talk, Mom," Eliza said. "It's the way Dad talks." Eliza took a container of Rainbow Meal Worms out of the icebox and opened it. "It's time to feed the frog," she said.

"Okay," I said. "I'll do the water."

"These are dead," she said, poking the worms. "He won't eat them."

"Maybe they're just cold. They might revive when they warm up. Let's try 'em." I took the worms from her and put a few in the cage.

Now Eliza was back reading and Hank was running water.

I looked under the sink and discovered we were out of Spic and Span. Then I looked at the frog cage and I noted that warming up the worms hadn't help enliven them. We had learned a few things about frogs, in addition to the fact that they like live food, since we started keeping them. It's true, for example, based on this household's experience, that if you give a tree frog too many worms, he goes on a hunger strike and the worms lie around in the grass in the cage and get warm and hatch into beetles and crawl up and down the plastic sides and ceiling of the cage.

I went to bed and lay there. The sheets were twisted,

and that annoyed me, but I didn't fix them. They were wearing out, too, and so was my nightgown, I noticed. If my aunt could see me now, she'd tell me that ragman story, I thought. It's a good story, actually, about the ragman who lived in a town that was once lively but had lately grown solemn and silent because a powerful, sneaky murderer was killing off all the townspeople, one by one. Every morning a new murder was discovered.

It didn't take very long before there was no one left in the town except the ragman and the murderer. And night was coming.

The ragman dragged himself through the streets, past the boarded-up dentist's office (for there was no more dentist), past the barber pole tumbling down (because there was no more barber to set it straight), past the town clock with the wrong time (for the town time-keeper had also met his doom). On the empty corner near his house, the ragman met the murderer, but the murderer passed him by with a look of disgust on his face.

"Why not me?" inquired the ragman, looking the murderer full in the eye. He was almost pleading.

"Okay, okay," said the murderer, and he rolled up his sleeves and settled his fat fingers around the scrawny neck of the ragman and began to choke him. But no matter how hard the murderer choked, he couldn't do away with the ragman. "What's the matter with you?

Why aren't you dead yet?" spit out the murderer. "Because I'm a ragman," whined the ragman. On hearing that he had been tricked into trying to kill a bunch of rags, the murderer became desperate with rage and wept and screamed and carried on all night and finally hanged himself. But the ragman just slumped on home through the empty town, entirely alone, entirely safe.

I heard the dishwasher go on, and then I picked up *The New York Review of Books* and turned to the article on abortion and was about halfway through by the time Hank came in. He was carrying a bottle of wine and two glasses.

"I think we should have a drink," he said.

"No thanks," I said. "Wine makes me sick. I haven't been drinking wine for at least four years. I know you remember," I said. Why was he trying this? He set the wine on the night table. Unopened. I stared at it and talked while I was staring. "You know, I really don't know what my favorite color is and I don't know what I like to eat anymore and I don't think there is anything I have an opinion on that isn't your opinion."

He was lining up his loafers in the closet. "You're exaggerating, *sashimi*," he said.

"What?"

"Japanese endearment."

"Really. Don't you think that's odd?"

He didn't say anything. He was undressing.

"Aren't you going to take off your nightgown?" he said. He was shaking out his slacks.

"I'm cold."

"Well, at least take off your underpants." He held his slacks away from him and looked through one leg of the slacks to the floor.

I took off my underpants and I threw them at his feet. In Eliza's teeth trick, who is supposed to hear that sound, the person making it or the person listening for it?

"You know what I would really like," I said.

"What would you like?" he said.

"A pair of pajamas. I used to wear pajamas. I had a pair of white pajamas with red piping. They were great."

"I don't like you in pajamas."

"I know you don't. That's why I don't have my red pajamas with white piping anymore. No, the other way around. Red piping on white pajamas." He was under the covers on his side now, adjusting the things on his night table. I continued: "I was just thinking, actually. While I sleep tonight, my nightgown is going to bunch up around my neck and choke me. It's been like this for eight years."

"You've been choking for eight years?"

"*Strangled*'s a better word."

"You should stop buying those things. You know I

don't like you to wear anything. Such a childish thing you do, cover yourself up against me. I'm married to an eight-year-old."

"There's your proof, then."

"What do you mean?"

"Eight-year-olds don't have affairs." I closed my eyes and put my arms down at my sides and lay there, very, very straight. He rolled toward the window, reached for the light, and turned it off.

"Do you know there are hardly any doors in our house?" I said.

"What about doors?" he said.

"Nothing."

"Do you want to make love?" he said.

"No," I said.

"What do we need them for, then?"

"Green," I said. "Green is my favorite color."

"You're going to have to grow up, Kate. I need to make love. It settles me. Besides, it's the way I feel close to you. It's the way I show you I love you."

"I know," I said. "Tomorrow," I said.

I was up early next day, looking out the front windows. The sun was coming up through the trees. There was an old man swinging on a swing in the playground. He was dragging one foot on the ground, scraping the toe of his shoe. He was the only person in that part of the park.

Farther on, where the road cut through the park, there were runners, and beyond that the tennis courts, unready, patchy with blackened snow and pools of water. I was watching the old man swing when Eliza brought me her hairbrush and the news that there wasn't enough sugar in her cocoa. She said she didn't like her egg and besides it was cold because she had to hunt for her picture of her bear called Richard—the picture she took before Richard lost his leg (last fall). She wanted to put the picture on her bulletin board. She said she thought the leg was somewhere in the country house because when we were in the driveway leaving the country house she asked to go back and get the leg, and Hank had said, In the spring.

We were late for the school bus. We rushed downstairs and to the corner. The sidewalks were slush. Eliza had no boots on. I let it go. On the way back I bumped smack into Jack Cardiff. In response he flattened against a building wall.

"Something on your mind?" he said.

I told him that the tiles in my dining room were taking over my life. There was something wrong with them and I couldn't get them to look right.

"What's underneath the tiles?" he said.

"I don't know what's underneath," I said.

· · ·

The following Friday Eliza had a sleepover on the other side of town. I took her and then I cooked dinner and after dinner I switched my place at the table so I could look at Hank directly. He always turns his head toward the Cropsey, so I put myself in front of it. The Cropsey is the one valuable thing we have. It was a marriage gift from my aunt, the remaining legacy of my grandparents. Cropsey is one of those Hudson River School painters inclined to the dramatic. The one we have is a flagrantly pompous naturescape—water, tidal marshes, big weather, some cows.

I was thinking I would ask Hank if he wanted to become a Friend of the Ballet because then we could get first crack at getting tickets to *The Nutcracker*—we had messed up this year. Instead I asked him if he had ever wondered what was underneath the tiles on the floor.

"No, and don't get any ideas. The house looks fine."

"Okay," I said. Then I went right ahead and told him I had thought about our conversation the other evening and I had thought that even though it was true I was not having an affair and there was no reason for me to get a divorce—there was no one else, I said—I had thought about it a lot and I thought that I really wanted to be alone. "I like it better living alone," I said.

The statement just floated in the air. It had absolutely no weight, or even any credibility. For myself, I knew I had said it just then only because Eliza wasn't there and wouldn't be able to hear. He said he didn't want to think about breaking up a marriage, didn't want to have to worry about it. How could I do this to him? He was trying to get his work done. He had so much work to do and he was trying to support the family.

I reminded him he had told me the other night that he was preoccupied with me, and maybe now that he knew what was on my mind, he wouldn't have to be preoccupied. It was out in the open, it would be easier.

"We can face it squarely," I said. He looked past me at the cows in the Cropsey. He was a big man, a heavy body, sunk into itself.

"Why didn't you tell me this the other night?"

"Because you asked me if there was anyone else, and there wasn't. And you asked me if I was planning anything, and I wasn't. It was only later that I realized there was still something wrong, and even though I could tell you no to your two questions, I still didn't want to live with you, knowing there's no reason for wanting not to be married."

"You're confusing me, Kate," he warned.

"I want to be alone," I said again.

"You should be working toward building our marriage, not destroying it," he said.

"I've tried being married now for eight years and I don't like it."

"You're destroying what we have. You're not making plans for us. I'm making plans for us. I'm going to take you to Florence next fall, and you're looking at me and saying you want to be alone."

His face was fuller than it used to be and it was turning to pudding. It was an innocent face now, without treachery. What had happened? Where was the great daunting figure with the live eyes? In the office, I remembered, he could come down on you like an arrow. A blur of intent. No fear. Did he still do that? And to whom? At home, he thudded his way through to me, a cartoon bear, graceless and slow, offering company where none was sought, offering overperfumed flowers.

He swallowed some coffee. "I don't want to hear about this anymore," he said.

"I know this is painful. It's painful for me too, which is why I haven't been quite able to bring this up."

"You don't want to have a successful marriage, or a successful career or successful children. You're going to ruin everything because you just like to ruin things. What kind of life do you think Eliza is going to have with you dropping things where you please?

"Anyway, what difference does it make? There isn't enough money. Where could I live? I have to live here. So neither one of us is going to get what we want. I won't get a loving marriage and you won't get to be alone. Is that the way you want it? Well, that's what you're going to have. And don't think I'm going to let you off easy." His voice had a rip in it, the words torn from something caught inside him, from a knot of phlegm. He started coughing. It sounded threatening. To him or to me? A hurt, startled look came into his eyes.

"Your cold is much worse," I said.

He left the table in one motion. He coughed all the way down the hall. I followed after him.

I found him in the sitting room, emptying the 33⅓-rpm record album shelves. Without looking up he said he was going to throw out a lot more records and also a lot of stuff from his desk. I retrieved some of the Christmas music records and stacked them next to me. Don't do that, I said to myself as I did it. He said, "Why are you taking those records? They aren't yours."

"Yes, but if you were throwing them out, I thought you wouldn't mind."

He said, "The best thing for children is to grow up in a loving marriage. You are going to destroy your daughter."

"This is not one of those loving marriages," I said. "This is a case of something else altogether. We have no right to make her part of us. She can't possibly grow this way. You and I are dying on the inside. It just doesn't show yet. Inside we are stalks."

He handed me a record, as if giving me an invitation to say more.

I said: "We have no resiliency. We are milkweed. We are like the milkweed Eliza tries to make bows out of."

"Make sense, Kate."

"You've seen her. At Whitby Cove. Every time she tries to string milkweed the twig snaps. Or if it doesn't snap then, it snaps when she tries to draw an arrow through the string. Her room in the country is full of snapped twigs and loose string she won't throw out. You've noticed them. You said they look like an old person's neck because the strings hang like wattles. Remember, you explained to her what wattles were." I put my hand under my chin and pinched and vibrated the skin a little. Stay with it, don't wander off, I coached myself. But I didn't stay with it. I put my hand down and I said, "I think you need some antibiotics this time. That's some cough you have."

"You've given me a terrible headache. I don't know how we're going to get the taxes done tomorrow," he said.

We were quiet in bed. He slept. He woke and swallowed cough medicine he had already portioned out into the bottle cap and coughed and made clattering noises with his bedside things and opened the window some more and threw off the covers onto me.

Later on, he was hugging me. When he realized what he was doing, he got up and walked around some and came back to bed.

As soon as light came through the window, I took a shower. We have a powerful showerhead in our house. It really makes you concentrate on what you're doing. It's direct. I was completely wet in a jiffy.

When it was time to do the taxes we couldn't do the taxes because the accountant had our original notes, which I had sent him months ago so we could pay our estimated taxes. I went to the grocery store. All I could think to buy was fizzwater. On the way back I picked up Eliza.

The building intercom was ringing when we walked in the door. Grocery delivery. "It's the seltzer," I said.

"Just seltzer?" Hank said.

"It's a lot of seltzer. Six cases."

"What are we going to do with six cases? Where are we going to put seventy-two bottles of seltzer? This kitchen cannot accommodate seventy-two quarts at one time. What were you thinking of?"

"I don't know. I just saw them there and it was two for ninety-nine cents and so I got six cases. What do you mean, what was I thinking of. You know what I was thinking of."

Eliza answered the door. It was my favorite delivery

boy, the one with a few missing teeth and such a goofy smile. There was a cat lying in a big curl around his shoulders, a live orange cat with a small head and pale eyes.

"There's an animal on your neck," warned Hank.

"Can I touch him?" said Eliza.

"Her," said the delivery boy.

"No," said Hank.

"Just a minute," said the delivery boy. He made a few more trips to the hall and back to the kitchen. He put his hands on his shoulder, cupping the cat. "Is it okay?" he said to Hank. Eliza was already reaching.

"Please," said Eliza.

"Okay," said Hank.

"I'm looking for a home for her. She's the last one," he said.

"Oh," said Eliza, sitting down, instantly at one with the pretty fur ball.

"I don't think this is the right time to get a cat," I said.

"Of course it is," said Hank. "What a sweetheart this cat is, what a great pet, don't you think so, Kate?"

"Of course it is," I said.

It was only about five minutes more before she and the delivery boy, whose name was Jesse, had gone back to the store to get food and litter and other necessaries.

He helped set everything up, and when he left, the delivery boy said, "One of her brothers might have had worms. So you probably should get her checked."

Hank, being Hank, already had his coat on. "I know all about cats," he said. "Of course she'll have a thorough checkup. Right away, skipper." He saluted the delivery boy while calling out, "Eliza, get my canvas bag with the zipper. It's in the front closet." Then, to me, "Kate, do you think we could prevail on you to loan us one of your towels?" I retreated to fumble in the back linen closet. Hank was still at the door with Eliza, saying again that he knew all about cats and he would teach us. It would be a great pet. "What are you going to call her, Eliza?" he asked her.

"Cranny."

"Cranny?"

"Cranny."

"Why Cranny?"

"She looks cranny."

"Do you mean she looks like she knows a lot without having to learn it?"

"Right."

"That's *canny,* Eliza. The word is *canny.* No *r.*"

"I'm calling her Cranny."

"Are you sure?" I had reappeared with a forest-color hotel-weight towel.

"I'm sure."

"The word *cranny* means a little hiding place," Hank said.

"Her name is Cranny," said Eliza.

"Okay, Cranny. *Sa ikimasho,* let's go." Hank took the cat and put her in his cloth bag and put the strap over his shoulder and his other arm on Eliza's shoulder and they went out the door together. I followed.

It was the first day of February and it had been a freaky, blizzardy afternoon with thunderstorms. Now there was an icy drizzle and it was cold and dark. We took the car. The cat and Eliza rode in the front with Hank, the cat in her soft bag on her hotel-weight towel, asleep on Eliza's lap.

Inside the ASPCA, we took the room-sized elevator, Eliza holding Cranny, the cat's head calmly poking out of her bag and her eyes quiet. Very soon we were among family groups, families united not against a single enemy but around a common pet.

It felt homey. We were all together with our pets and our cans from the vending machines. Excited, straining dog pets and their families were on one side of the room; cat people with their cats stayed on the other side. Near the window there was a large family grouped around a bunny in a baby blanket. Lights flickered over us all. Every now and then one of the clerks reminded us: "If you're just picking up your pet, you don't have to wait in line. Everyone else needs a number." Hank tore off a number from a contraption like the ones in old-fashioned bakeries.

A vet came into the waiting room from behind glass doors. She was dressed in belted, loose khaki pants, her long-sleeved eggplant T-shirt tucked in, sensible shoes, identification plastic hanging from waist, stethoscope around neck. She explained to the receptionist that she was just out of the operating room and would help out with the routine cases now because she felt needed.

There was a general feeling of goodness, tolerance, solicitude, even, of people being nice to their pets and nice to one another.

On our side of the room, the conversations were about money and disease. There were cats with leukemia, heart failure, and asthma, and there were cats that cost too much money to take care of, but were worth it. I looked over my row and concentrated on the variety and styles of temporary cat housing: there were cages; blue plastic boxes; trunks with tops like double-decker skylight buses on city tours; two bags, one fancy, like a baby bag with a special cat-breathing screen; and a cardboard box.

Our seats faced the windows. It was bat-black outside but a generous supply of streetlamps made it almost as bright as day. We were close to the entrance to two bridges that leave the island. The highway was lit up and the bridges were lit up and it was a hub of departure preparations: limousines waiting to take people places, a car wash, buses at the end of their route or at the beginning of their route.

"Where are we?" Eliza wanted to know. I told her.

She looked out the big hole of a window to the light on the river and followed the highway lights across the bridge. She said, "I could get someplace from here," and settled back in her chair, whispering to her cat. Hank twisted his Bugs Bunny pen, a gift from the Japanese, and read.

The family with the rabbit stepped back into the elevator. The elevator door closed. It was our turn with our cat, our cat with skinny head and not much hair. Tufts of her hair invaded the nose of the vet, however, who pointed out Cranny's large, square bald spot and an uneven scar on the front right leg, and asked if we wanted to give Cranny some preemptive worm medicine. Hank said yes.

Through her speckled glasses, the vet peered into Cranny's ears, delicately stretching the skin this way and that to get a better view. She said she thought the bald spot might be either ringworm or mites. She gave Eliza a little plastic vial of medicine to put in the cat's ears three times a week, adding instructions to take the bottle out of the refrigerator a few hours before applying the drops so they wouldn't feel too cold, and to massage the drops into Cranny's ears before she shook it all out. I asked what ringworm looked like. "It looks like flaky sores," the vet said.

That night Hank went downtown to his Japanese-culture study group. He came back late and banged around for a while and got into bed. He said, to the ceiling: "Eight years . . ." And again, "Count them, one, two, three, et cetera. . . . For eight whole years I have had your legs in my legs. You never say anything about that. . . . I guess women get used to feeling balls and cocks on their bodies. . . . You're weak, Kate. . . . All my women have been weak." I held my breath until he curled away from me.

He got sick in the middle of the night. He turned on the lights to confirm that his hands really were swollen and it wasn't just the way he felt. He wanted me to look at his hands with him. They were swollen, or one hand was swollen. We waited together until morning and then, holding his hand, he went straight to his internist. He had pulled a muscle while carrying his extra-heavy briefcase.

If we had come together at all now, it would have been over the cat. But we did not come together.

The winter was interminable.

Hank said he was leaving and then he forgot all about leaving. He began to worry about the placement of paintings in the house. He held the cat. He taught her to dance with him. He praised her. He said he wanted to find the modem and attach it to the computer so he could talk to his department secretaries. He said he needed a fancy phone to do this. He ordered one. He started hanging family pictures in the kitchen. He wanted to make an appointment with me so we could rearrange the books, by subject. He began planning a trip to Lake Como, where we had gone on our honeymoon.

The back-and-forth escalated. He said he was never going to leave. He threw out books so he would have less to take with him when he left. He said, "This is the worst, that you should want to separate now." He said, "I'm glad I brought this on, because you've been so awful to me since the day I married you." He said, "I don't want Eliza to have a stepfather." I said, "She's not going to have a stepfather." He said, "You'll probably marry again. You'll be someone else's third wife."

He laughed, now and then. He whistled in the halls. He still showed up in the bedroom naked after a shower.

He laughed when our pets died, and they were always dying, though we still had one frog and one hamster left from creatures that I had taken in serially, with the idea that this was the natural way to learn about life and death. When I complained about his attitude toward the animals, he pointed out that the animals had been useless anyway, that what Eliza learned about life and death was that worms hatch into beetles and that when a hamster dies, it dies on its back with one paw stuck straight in the air.

He said whatever came into his head in front of Eliza, things like "We're not going to be able to send you to school next year because your mother is making our lives difficult." I did not want to counter him in front of Eliza because it seemed worse for her to hear us quarreling. So I was quiet and Eliza stood, also mute, hanging her head and later coming to me because an eye had come off her Raggedy Ann.

I tried to tell Hank about boundaries and children, how they can't take in bad news about their parents without thinking it's their fault, how their pets are really substitute selves. He said he didn't know about me, but that he and Eliza were not hamsters. He said I should stop reading whatever books I was reading.

He told me I better get a lawyer, because he had one.

He set up a bed in his study and moved in. I helped him. We told Eliza he had moved because he was working on a math problem and sometimes it woke him up and if he turned on the light I got too irritable the next day.

He was cheerful before bed, saying goodnight very politely in Japanese and whacking shut the door of his study. He kept his L. L. Bean miniature emergency light in there and his hot water bottle and his various digestive aids and sinus medications, including the one that smelled like a cool place in deep woods. One night he showed up suddenly in "my" bedroom, snapping on the light. He had something shiny in his hands. "You know what coming in here reminds me of?" he said. He was holding aloft the object, which I could see now was a pair of scissors. "It reminds me of when I was a boy and my mother went to the hospital to have another baby and I went into her closet and cut up her clothes. Snip. Snip. Snip." He echoed his announcement with four or five clicks of the scissors. Then he switched the light off and on and off again, left the room, came back, turned the light on once more so I'd have to get up to turn it off, and whistled himself back down the hall.

Eliza learned how to tell time but she couldn't keep it straight. She had a routine now of waking up at night and wandering in with the news "I'm not scared." I would lead her back to bed. She would come again and tell me the time. It was always the wrong time.

Hank became angry. He seemed angry all the time now. It was a way for him to pass the time. I never knew what was going to happen. We hardly ever went out all together anymore, and not at all after a wretched Sunday excursion to a new kind of bookstore in our neighborhood.

It was a "megastore bookmart," with a café and huge

escalators and many levels, and ceilings that felt higher than the Cathedral of Saint John the Divine, which gave me a feeling of sanctuary. It seemed like a place where people could be happy without bumping into one another, where we could each get absorbed.

On entering, Hank announced that he didn't want any more new books, so he took his own book he had been carrying and sat in the café. Eliza and I had a field day roaming the aisles. We came back to the café with our arms full of books and found Hank arguing with the waiter, who was insisting Hank order something if he wanted to stay.

I asked for ginger ale and coffee. We sat down to read. Hank leaned forward into his book. It was Philip Roth's *The Facts*. He was near the end, where the countervoice comes in and says maybe the narrator's life is a mess because he purposefully married a victim. Maybe he had his own problems and he let her act out for him and then condemned her. Maybe she was his true inspiration for all of his work. I knew that's where he was because I had marked that part in yellow and I could see the yellow from where I was sitting.

Hank suddenly began pounding the book with his fist. He had it open and he may have broken the spine. Then he got up and went to a trash can and forced the book in, jamming it through the opening. Other trash fell out as he did this.

"What's wrong?" said Eliza.

"He's angry," I said.

"Why?"

"It's not you," I said.

I didn't know what to do. I took her for a walk to Audio Books, a long way away.

"Why is he so angry?" she said after a while.

"He doesn't want to talk about it, but it's not you. Maybe it's the book."

"He was angry before he was reading the book," she pointed out.

"Well, I guess he's worried about his work."

She didn't answer me. We were almost back where we started, and we could see that he was gone.

His comings and goings became erratic, or at least at odds with what he announced before leaving the house. One night, when I was going to a benefit with my friend Jane, he was a half hour late coming home. The babysitter had left early because she had a date. Eliza and I were playing a game in the sitting room. It's called Headache and it involves clickers that sound like a cricket in your ear. It gave me a sore head to hear the clickers, but I had to keep clicking because that was the way the board pieces moved, a click and then the dice twirled to say how many spaces to move. Eliza said she wanted to watch television. I said, Not on a weekday.

She said she hated me. I said, I know it makes you mad. She said, This is a special night. My dad is cooking me spaghetti and meatballs.

"I know it's special but you can't watch TV." She cried. She said that everything was ugly in our house.

"What is ugly?"

"My dad's study is ugly. It has a big bed sticking out of the wall."

"Lots of studies have beds in them," I said.

"Not a big bed like that, with white pillows. It looks stupid."

I couldn't think.

"I want to watch TV," she said again.

"Let's finish this game," I said.

"I hate you," she said.

"I know you hate me, but I know you love me too, and you love me more than you hate me. Your hate can't wipe out your love. And I love you too." She rolled away from me on the floor.

"Hate," she said.

"Love," I said.

"Hate," she said. She banged an empty magazine rack on the floor. It hardly made a sound. "Hate," she said. Then, "Where is a guest going to sleep?"

"The guest can sleep in the sitting room on the day-bed."

"What if two guests want to spend the night?"

"One can sleep in your top bunk."

"That's where Cranny sleeps. It's Cranny's bed."

"Both guests can sleep in my bed, then."

She seemed somewhat placated by the idea. We finished the game. She won. She had all the pieces, one on top of another, which was the point of the game. She rolled over again and banged the magazine stand. "Hate," she said softly, and the corners of her mouth angled like tricycle handlebars and she looked at me without turning her head, so that her cold eye was level with the tangle of her hair and I saw a young woman in love, moaning the word "hate."

The door opened and Hank was there, untangling his umbrella strap from his coat and saying "*Komban wa*, good evening," without seeing us. I didn't answer but looked at him and he looked back and said, "What?" and I said, "You said you would be home at seven."

"So I'm fifteen minutes late."

"It's after seven-thirty."

"Well, the sitter is here until eight."

"She had to go out."

He blew up. I don't remember the words. "You unnerve me," that was one thing he said. The rest was lost in a huge blot. He kept coming back to me, pointing his finger at me and poking my arm. I was trying to get away, putting on lipstick, looking for my hairbrush, tiptoeing around the house, hoping his yelling would

end. Eliza was following too, saying, "It's not his fault."
I said nothing except "It's okay. It's okay."

Eliza asked if she could watch TV. "Ask your father,
he's in charge now," I said. But she was scared to ask
him and asked me to ask him and I did and he said, Sure.
I left her sitting in front of the TV, watching Yogi Bear.
Hank was in the kitchen, slamming things and striding
back and forth, and out in the hall, telling me to hurry
up and leave.

In the morning, Eliza came in and said she had been
scared last night. "I was too," I said.

"You shouldn't have gotten angry at him," she said.

"I'm going to try not to disturb him again," I said.

This was all wrong. But it was early in the morning.

Hank found an apartment, not nearby but close, in a
way, to his family. It was his first wife's apartment. She
was living with his best friend now. He said he might
have a job in Japan.

I got a lawyer. I told the lawyer I wanted a no-fault
divorce if it came to divorce, but for now I simply
wanted to live alone. The lawyer told me to get all my
files in order so when we got to a distribution of prop-
erty I would know what was what.

When I came home I was crying. "Your tears are
water," Hank said.

The weather improved.

Hank wanted to make love. I didn't refuse. I was tired of being mean. It was exhausting. I did whatever he wanted me to do. It was convenient to be kind. He didn't ask for much and I would have felt ridiculous refusing. Yet I didn't want to encourage him. It seemed to be one of those times when you are supposed to go against all normal impulses and actually make an effort to be mean. I hoped, I guess, that he would do the work for me. If I said the right thing, the right annoying thing, he might start throwing dishes at me.

He wouldn't do that. He held out. Exhaustion was part of his strategy, and his fortitude was impressive. Besides, he had stopped opening my mail and making fun of my thumbs. I began to think, There are a lot of things I like about this person I don't want to be with, and after a while I couldn't even remember why I wanted to be divorced.

At the same time, I felt completely flattened by him when he was in the house, as if I were a road and he were a shadow on it. When he wasn't at home, when no one was, in the daytime, when I was supposed to be working, I sat in my study with my comforter over me, sat in the falling-apart wicker chair, looking at the flag out my window, trying to think up a good enough reason for messing up people's lives, trying to tell myself there never is a good enough reason when the other person is looking in the other direction. I was waiting to feel strong and clear and trying to really believe that no one could help me, especially not my husband. What I felt was blank, fretted, like the flag stuck to the pole, as if I were in a prison movie, plotting a break while having lunch with the warden. Being on my own seemed more and more of a dream.

Part of it had to do with not being able to tell Eliza, because Hank wasn't actually leaving.

One afternoon, I was on my way to get my teeth cleaned, talking to myself. Is there a law that says you have to love your husband to stay married? Would it really be better for Eliza to go on like this inside this shell of a family? And what about the tiles. What kind of a woman spends her whole married life in a house in which the dining room is covered with black and white linoleum squares and never even wonders what's underneath the squares?

In my mind, I was pulling up the tiles, one black, one white, one black. They resisted. I kept pulling. The floor was coming up with the tiles. It was rotten.

"Come on. It couldn't be bad as all that." It was Jack Cardiff in his tennis clothes. He was carrying little packages in a sack. Varieties of fruit. I imagined he must have picked out each one in each little group. There was a nice, finished look about him and his packages and his legs.

"I think I'm having my midlife crisis," I told him. He

admired my raincoat. "It's all that's holding me together," I said.

He called later with "a short bulletin: Do you know that the whole rest of the world doesn't know what it's doing most of the time? Sometimes I think you don't know how well you do. You're really very competent, and the fact that you fall down the stairs sometimes is okay. If you listen, you hear the sound of people thudding down the stairs all the time."

"There's a shadow over me," I told the phone. "I can't shake it."

"Honey," he said. "Where are you now?"

I didn't answer. I was under my comforter.

"Are you there?" I heard a soft voice, a comfort-food voice, tender, liquid, and warm.

"Yes," I said.

"Honey," he said again. "You're going to get out, but it will take a little time."

I had a brief understanding that there was not a lot of feeling at the center of this voice, that there was something held back about it. But what I kept remembering from this conversation was that he called me honey.

He called the next day, and the next, always before he had to be somewhere, with brief messages, about the weather, about credit-card interest rates, about the state of the auto industry. He didn't call me honey. The rhythm in his voice, traveling unaccompanied and vibrating through the wires, had a low, reverberating pitch, an anchoring quality. I began to look forward to the sound of Jack's voice.

One morning, before he left for work, Hank said the painting was finished in his ex-wife's apartment and he might move out over the next few weeks. I said I thought that was a good idea. I said, "In any case, let's tell Eliza we are separated."

"When do you want to tell her?"

"Tonight," I said.

After he left, I went back to bed and lay down. It was the third day of darkness in the morning. But there was wind, and the darkness began to lift, to a gray-white. A cold dullness. I got up.

I had research to do in the library. When I came home, Eliza and the baby-sitter were playing cards. Eliza was in good spirits. She ran to greet me: "Who goes there with the brown, brown hair," she said and jumped at me and ran back to play. I boiled some water for tea and sat in the kitchen holding the warm cup in both hands, watching the clock. At twenty-seven after seven, the front door opened and Eliza ran to it and said, "Who goes there with the short white hair?" It was her dad and they yelped at each other for a few moments and she went back again to play.

He changed his clothes and came into the kitchen and

said a few things to me, but I didn't hear them because the water was running and because I had my mind on something else. I gave him his messages, the most important one being about his dinner later that evening with his colleagues and visiting Japanese bank officials at the Japanese consulate.

He asked about Eliza. "She seems awfully cheerful, shame to interrupt her."

"I think we should interrupt her," I said.

"Maybe we should take the printer apart instead."

"I don't think so. Not now."

"I thought you said it was broken."

"It is broken, but I fixed it, temporarily. I can print one page at a time. That's good enough until we can get a new platen, and we can't do that tonight." Then, "I think we should interrupt Eliza."

"Up to you," he said. He poured her some orange juice and we went into the sitting room and we called her. She said she was busy, and then I went to her room and said, "Come. We want to talk with you for a little while." She and the baby-sitter were finishing a card game. The baby-sitter had the full deck in her hands and she told Eliza she would set up a new game after she talked with us. So Eliza bounded out of her room and we three sat down.

"What do you want to talk about?" she said.

"About how we are together," I said.

"I know all about that," she said.

She was sitting on the arm of the sofa between Hank and me, and he handed her a cracker. I began again: "You know how your father sleeps in one room and I sleep in another?"

"Yes."

"And often we don't go out together?"

"Yes."

"And often he goes away and comes back?"

"Yes."

"That's called separating. We're separating from each other, a little at a time."

And Hank said, tactfully, I thought, "But we're not separating from you." He took her hand and I took her other hand with the cracker still in it, and he said again, "Do you see? We'll never separate from you."

"I know that." She was impatient, but she could see we weren't about to let her go.

"I wish Dad wasn't in that room. I have no place to put my dolls when they need a change."

"Maybe you could put them in my room for a few days. But you'd have to take them out after that."

"That's the problem. I don't want to take them out."

"Maybe you could put them in the pantry," I said.

"There's no bed in there," she said.

Hank said, "We could get rid of your play sink and stove and make room for a little bed." She seemed agreeable to that. Neither one had noticed that her play sink and stove weren't there anymore, hadn't been for a few months. I said nothing.

"Eliza, when people are separating, sometimes there are arguments and loud voices. The arguments aren't about you," I said.

"I know. Jeanie's parents are like that. They're divorced. Her father's coming back in May."

I understood then that we hadn't made a dent, but I didn't feel too bad because it was a start. I said, "I thought you might get worried if you heard things you didn't understand."

"I'm not worried. Can I go now?"

Hank said, "If you have any questions, you ask either your mother or me. We'll answer you."

"I know," she said. She wanted to leave.

"Do you have any questions now," he said.

"How much is thirty and a hundred and thirty?" she said seriously, and then laughed and rolled back on her legs and looked at each of us and ran out of the room.

She ate her dinner and played more cards and took a bath, and when she got out, she wanted some animal crackers and milk and a few stories. The last story we read was the theater program from *Snow White on Ice*. She thought the picture of Snow White in the glass coffin with her ice skates on was pretty funny.

She fell asleep with no problem. I kept busy for a

while hemming napkins. When Hank came back, he reported that the Japanese food was the best he had ever had. He rubbed his stomach and went off to bed.

Eliza woke up happy. She could not be coaxed into wearing her winter coat even though it was a cold day and the class was going on a trip on the Staten Island Ferry and all the children had been told to dress warmly.

Hank said he thought the talk with her had gone pretty well. He noted that Eliza was carrying on much as usual. "I guess it doesn't matter to her much," he said. I should have said, "I don't think she gets it yet," but I didn't. I was thinking about what he might do to try to make it matter to her.

Eliza had more to say when she came home from school. First a hug. Then, "Mom, why don't you have a baby? You only had one. I want you to have two."

"I can't have another baby because your father and I are separating and when married people separate, they don't have babies together anymore."

"You're not separating. You're both here. You go out to different places and Dad goes away on trips. Lots of dads do that. You're not divorcing."

"Our lives are more and more apart. We're separating from each other but not from you. Parents don't ever separate from children." (Thank you, Hank.)

"You're separating from me. I hate you."

"I know you're mad about all this. That's—"

"You don't even know why I'm mad at you."

"Why are you mad at me?"

"I'm not telling you." Pause. "You don't give Cranny any treats."

"You don't think I take good care of her?"

"She needs a new toy."

"What kind of new toy?"

"I don't know. We need to choose."

"Let's choose one the next time we go grocery shopping. Good idea?" I said.

"Okay," she said. She picked up Cranny and burrowed her head in the cat's tummy. She stroked her. She hugged her. She looked happy. She said, "You're not separating."

"We are separating."

"You're living together in the same house."

"Someday we won't all live together. You're going to live with me."

"I'm not going to live here with you. I'm living with my dad. Why does he have to live somewhere else?"

I couldn't think why.

"I want it to be like the old days," she said.

"Things move ahead. You can't go backward. We'll go slowly and we won't do anything until we're all comfortable."

"I'm comfortable here, with you in the afternoon and Dad coming home at night."

"You want to go backward?"

"I want to do the old things tomorrow. And the day after tomorrow. And the day—"

"Okay, I hear you," I said.

"On Tuesday, my dad is going to make me a hamburger. You never make me hamburgers. Never in your life. You don't know how."

"He's very good at hamburgers. Should I try too, or maybe I could make you something else?"

"Noodle soup."

"Yes, I'll make that."

Hank and I were in the kitchen. It was the weekend again. We had been in the house too long together. It was once again a stormy day. He said, "I wish I had known from the beginning that you didn't love me."

Forgetful Jones, I thought. We weren't supposed to love each other in the beginning.

I said, "Maybe you married me so you could get away from feeling old." I was surprised to hear myself talking out loud.

He said, "Stop that."

I said, "Maybe you worried you were dying and you wanted fresh blood around you. Thought it might liven you up. But I can't—"

He menaced me with a boiling kettle. A sharp escalation. "I told you to stop that," he said again.

"Then stop insulting me. Don't tell me whether I love. Don't talk to me about my motives. I had the same motives you had. You gave them to me, remember? Blockhead?"

"I'm not insulting you," he said, almost tenderly, but with an obscene smile. He had seen me flinch.

"Just don't tell me how I feel," I said again.

"I won't. I'm not." Then, "Look, I give up."

"What?"

"I said, 'I give up.' "

"Give up what?"

"You're right about us, Kate. We have no marriage. I should never have married you." The kitchen felt crowded now. It felt crowded and it was too quiet. Hank broke the silence, but so flatly it took me a few moments to hear him. He said, "You used to look so much like her. Before Eliza was born."

"I used to look like Eliza?"

"Your mother. You used to look so much like your mother. The first time you walked into my off—"

"You mean my aunt? That's rude, Hank. You know I was never fat."

"Kate, I knew your mother. You didn't know your mother, but I knew your mother. I knew her before you were born."

"What are you talking about?"

"In Whitby Cove. She had a little money, from your grandparents, I guess, and she rented a cottage near ours and she lived there the summer before you were born, the summer she was carrying you. She was by her—"

"Why are you saying these crazy things?"

"—self. Just listen. I got to know her because she was on my paper route and she used to make fresh lemonade for me. She was the only one on my route that ever offered me a drink."

I said, "I'm busy. Go away."

He said, "And we used to talk. I was eleven. She couldn't have been more than ten years older than me. But she had already lived her life, it turned out." I had a picture in my head now of a young girl, about the size of Eliza, but pregnant. She was bouncing a pink ball and talking to herself, "*A* my name is Alice . . ."

I said again, "Go away, Hank." Hank was in my picture now, an outrageous cliché of a grown man in a raincoat watching my mother bounce her ball.

"I'm not going away," Hank said.

"Please go away."

"No."

"Okay. You are saying to me, out of the blue, after all these years of not saying it, and you want me to believe it, that you knew my mother, my dead mother?"

He had that silly ostrich look on his face, as if any minute he were going to hide his head in the sand.

"Yes."

"So why haven't you told me this before?"

"It was too weird. Besides it was corny. I had such a crush on her. But I'm telling you now. I knew Alice. Your mother was a very, very beautiful woman. Not very tall. In fact she was only a little bigger than the pond ferns. She'd get lost in them. The loosestrife towered over her."

"Loosestrife?"

"That purply stuff. Fragile, light-looking. It attracts white butterflies. I was taller than she was. That was the year I grew six inches."

"Nobody grows six inches in a year."

"Yes, they do. That's typical of you, to say something like that now."

"What should I say, Hank?"

"Don't you care, aren't you curious about your own mother?"

"If I want to know about my own mother, I'm not going to ask a stranger, especially one who makes up such dumb lies."

"Okay, don't ask. Sit down. I'm going to tell you."

I made for the door but he blocked it with his frame and with the kettle, which he was still holding. He pulled the little top open with his trigger finger. I took a seat on the windowsill, but not before I had tripped over the garbage can pedal. The red door of the can lifted. I let it stay that way.

"Put down the lid," he said.

"Put down the kettle," I said.

We both obeyed.

"Ask me about your mother," he said.

I pressed my lips together.

"It wasn't just that she was nice to me about lemonade. It wasn't even how she looked, or how you looked, for that matter. It was, you know what happened, before I actually saw you something preceded you. I knew who you were before you told me who you were. It could be something chemical that's the same in you and Alice; maybe you just happened to be using the same toothpaste or perfume and that brought up the first thing I remember about your mother, which was, the first thing I remember was the way she smelled—a lightness like sweetbrier and marshes and tim—"

"Is that why I have all that Chanel?"

"Yes. It's not quite the same on you."

"Hank, this is completely fishy and completely cuckoo. One of your really stupid, idiotic lies. It's like hiding in plain sight. Why are you doing this now?"

"I don't know why."

"This is such a mean time for you to go nuts," I said.

"It's not fair." I took a giant step out of the kitchen and stalked down the hall.

Eliza was at the far end of the hall, coming toward me. "Where's Dad?" she said.

"In the kitchen. Can't you hear him?" He was whistling "When the Moon Comes Over the Mountain."

"Come," she said. "It's a surprise for both of you." She and her little friend Jeanie collected Hank and led us down the hall toward the big bedroom. Hank was saying names of things, country things: "Timothy, salt marshes, sweet grass, catbrier, juni—" The children were laughing and chirping, and on my bed were flowers and shells and bouquets of fake flowers and little baskets with ribbons in them and silk-thread necklaces. He said, "Well, this is nice, but it isn't my room."

And then Jeanie said, "Why isn't this your room?" And he said, "This is Kate's room. I don't sleep here." And he showed her where he slept, across the hall, and Eliza flushed to her ears and was confused because she had forgotten or because she was embarrassed or because she had counted on us to protect her. We all stood there dumbly by the bed with its bouquets of paper flowers on it, and Jeanie said, "Why do you sleep in separate rooms?" and I said, "Because we are separated," and at the same time Eliza said, "Because my dad is working on a math problem."

"And because he's working on a math problem," I

added. Then quickly, "Let's go out, kids. We'll go to McDonald's. Dad's going to the movies."

"Don't you want to go to a movie? I'll take the children," Hank said.

"No. I'm hungry. Let's go, kids."

Later that night Jeanie cried because her father was in Saskatchewan and one brother was also far away and the other had had tooth surgery. And still later she pulled out one of her own teeth, and after that she fell asleep. I slept on the end of the bed for a while—they were both in my bed—and then I went into Eliza's bed and she came in later.

I had all night to think about Hank and my mother, but oddly I couldn't. My mother and Hank were not very real, or very relevant, they were somehow unrelated to me. In a way, they bored me. I didn't even know if I believed Hank, though the story was an odd one for him. Much too creative. Accepting it would require a complete rethinking of him, and I didn't feel like thinking anymore. It was just too late. It was over. And my mother, maybe it was that my mother had never seemed as if she could have been my mother. She was too small, too young, she was another child, like me, my sister. The idea I had about Alice was that she always asked permission to do things, and the one time she didn't, and took things into her own hands, well, that was me. I was her stab at liberty.

My aunt seemed my rightful mother. She was the right size and age and she was what a mother was supposed to be, sturdy, reliable, around in her apron. My aunt wore aprons in her kitchen and she was a terrible cook, especially her meat loaf, which she made with Wheaties. I thought about my aunt in bed and the crumpled-up Kleenex and the knobs on the radio and how many times I had to eat that meat loaf. No wonder I was unsentimental. There was no reason to be sentimental.

And I thought about Isabel. Isabel was more present and relevant to me than my mother or my aunt or Hank, Isabel on the bench last year in her pale cotton dress, her arms tenderly poking out of the sleeveless top, Isabel with her light brown eyes, saying "Bullshit." Isabel would give a paperboy a special homemade drink. She would teach him things. She would know about loose-strife and that business about white butterflies. Something about Isabel must have been in my mother too, something strong enough to get my unreal husband to try to resurrect her by marrying me. "Marry" meaning "murder." He'd have had to murder me first to get to her, wipe off all the crust, the traces of me, wipe me clean away. My murderous, arrogant, and possessive husband. Unforgivable. I guess. What difference. It hardly seemed worth the effort. All the mothers that counted, the mothers we wanted, were dead.

How I must have dimmed in his eyes when, little by little, I proved I was not Alice, whatever Alice was. How I must smell to him now.

I felt ashamed. I felt so sorry. I put my arms around myself. I tried to be tender, to hold on gently, to fall asleep.

The storm was still with us the following morning. I saw that from the front windows. I was up early, listening to it and watching it while I printed out a rewrite of a piece for the bank's magazine. I had decided to keep myself busy, but I was having trouble with the printer again.

The wind was still strong enough to keep the traffic light swaying. I pointed out the light to Hank after he came in and started closing the windows.

"It looks like a thurible," he said.

"A what?"

"Thurible. It's what priests use during benediction. It has incense in it. It's for blessings."

"How do you know about that?"

"Mary," he said. (His first wife.)

"Oh." I stared ahead at the bare trees, a pale disk on a stump halfway up a tree, the yellow slide, two squirrels, a hawk, a nest of hawks, high in the branches, off by itself.

"We don't have to get divorced. We could start again, Kate," he said.

"You're trying to trick me to get me to stay in the marriage," I said.

"No."

"What was she like, then?" I think both of us were watching the hawks.

"What was your mother like?"

"Who else?"

"In general?"

"Okay."

"Narrow like you. Narrow shoulders. Freckles. A lot shorter than you. I've already said that. Wonderful hands."

"Thumbs?"

"Perfect."

"What was she *like,* Hank?"

"You're screaming," he said. Then, "I don't know. I was just one of the kids in the neighborhood. I pulled weeds for her. I collected worms. I caught her a fish. She had one of those straw hats that cast a pattern over her face when the sun was on it. Latticework."

"Latticework."

"Yeah. Very peaceful person. Her place was on the glider and mine was the chair covered with flowers. I could think when I was with her."

I moved over to the printer and stuck a blank piece of paper in the tray. It went through crookedly and started to catch and rumple. Hank had followed me, still talking. "She had that special thing women have when they are really paying attention to you. She could be knitting, making her crochet things, but she would be thinking of me, I could feel her tuned to me. She made me feel like somebody. There was more to me when I was with her. Do you know what I mean?" He shut the printer off.

Outside, the wind howled. There was the awful sound of shovels on cement. Hank was still talking but I couldn't hear him. I didn't want to or I wasn't trying or the shovels really overpowered his voice. On our side of the street, there were big spaces of black where cars had pulled out. Across the street, the parked cars had snow packed up to the side windows past the rearview mirrors. The street plow had come through in the night.

"Are you making this up?" I said.

"No," he said.

"It's a whopping coincidence," I said.

"She noticed me, Kate. She knew me. Not one person in my house noticed how different it was for me when I suddenly got tall. I could hear better, see better, reach farther, hold on to things better than ever before. I could use a saw like a guy twice my size. I could pull that sucker without a ripple. And she knew it, she knew it before I knew it."

"One of those things where if a tree barks in the woods—"

"It's 'If a tree falls in the woods and no one hears it, did it really fall?' It's Berkeley's question, spelled Berkeley, pronounced Barkley. For God's sake, Kate, are you paying attention to me?"

"I am paying attention to you. I'm upset, okay? Besides, our tree frogs bark, or used to bark, when we had them."

Pause.

"I think about Alice every time I estimate. She was the one who showed me how to do it."

"Numbers? You're talking to me about numbers now?"

"Listen. She used to have me estimate what things would cost before I took the money out of her grocery jar. Later, when we were sitting around, we'd do it with six-digit numbers, round them and then reduce them so it would be something like 24 minus 17 instead of 236,439 minus—"

"I understand you."

"And it saved me. I hardly ever got anything wrong again, and I think about her every time I do it. That's what gets to me. It's such a habit that I do it without thinking. But then I think about her."

"How did she know that?"

"I told you, she *knew* things."

"They teach estimating in the second grade at Coventry."

"Not thirty years ago. Can you imagine what a gift that was to me? I never would have gone on in math if it hadn't been for her. Alice was my teacher."

"Did she look like Isabel?"

"Who?"

"Never mind. Is Eliza like her?"

"Not very. No." Then, "I thought you could learn to love me."

"You thought I could learn to love you."

"Yes. Because in a sense you had before. And I had loved you. You were part of her, after all."

"You hoped I would be my mother."

"Yes, I hoped that. I guess I hoped that."

"That's crazy."

"Lower your voice, Kate. I don't think it was so crazy. It was a risk, is all."

"It's not fair to take that kind of risk when the other side is blind."

"I didn't say it was fair. I said it was a risk. Anyway, it almost worked."

"Not for you," I said. "It didn't almost work for you."

"That's right. It didn't work for me. I wanted it to work. Look, I said I was sorry, Kate."

Pause.

"Do you want to hear more?" he said.

I didn't answer and he began talking to the window, about how it must have been the way her perfume worked into her skin and sent back something into the air around her, about how she "moved in her blossoming" (meaning me, I guess) as if the feminine were her territory alone. It sounded like a bunch of nonsense, actually, but the effect on me was that I began to feel like an imposter. It was a real fight for me to get a grip.

I at last said, "If I could just get you to admit things."

"What things?"

"About what a mess this whole thing is, Hank. A complete mess."

"It doesn't have to be. Look, let me tell you something Alice said, and don't butt in. She said, and she believed this, that there isn't anybody whose capacity for love is so slight he can't light up the whole city of Hartford with it." He hung his head and then began to raise it as the sound of his own words got to him. His eyes were running and he started to speak again but I cut across him.

"Okay, let's talk about Hartford. Did it ever occur to you that together we could never light up one lightbulb, never mind Hartford. Maybe, together, we cancel each other out. If you would talk just one minute to me about that, we might have some place real to start. If you would just talk to me about the loss that our marriage is. You must feel it too."

"We're talking, Kate."

"Yeah, but we're not really. We're not talking about you. You are the loss and I am the loss and I feel that you are forbidding me to talk about that. And what about Eliza? You think it's good for her to be in the dark we make ourselves?"

"I'm not forbidding anything. I just don't know what you're saying."

"If I mention it, like now, you look at me as if you suddenly realized you were going in the wrong direction, and the conversation doesn't get started. It's over."

"It doesn't have to be over, Kate. We could try again. Let's try again. Ours is not the first marr—"

"Yes, but it's mine."

"If you have me around, you won't get too caught up in Eliza. That's what isn't good for her."

"The reason I get 'too caught up,' as you call it, in Eliza is that you are around. I'm just trying to get away from you. You push me toward her."

"Okay," he said.

The subway underneath us rattled past. Which way? I couldn't tell.

"This marriage is wrong. I want it to end. You're using Eliza to make me stay."

"You have it backward again, Kate. You are using Eliza to try to get out of your marriage."

"The whole thing is wrong."

"Okay," he said.

"Anyway, we don't have time for this now. I want to get the printer fixed so I can do my work."

"You want to do that now? With me?" I had surprised him with my practicality.

"I don't want to talk, so we might as well keep busy."

"Call first and see if the place is open. I'm not driving up to the Bronx for nothing."

The parts place was open but I had to get the serial number of the platen so the girl on the phone could check part availability. The serial number was on the base of the platen, and I couldn't get the platen out of the printer. The girl suggested a man might be able to do it: "It's very delicate but you do need strength." On the next try, I still couldn't do it. She put me on hold and came back and said to look for the number near the bottom of the machine. I read that number out. "There's another number," she said.

"That's all the numbers there are," I said.

"Look again," she said.

Sure enough, there was a number on the side, but I couldn't read it because it was scratched out.

She got her boss on the line.

"I can't read the last number," I told him.

"You'll have to take out the platen."

"How do I do that?"

"Just pull straight up. It will come right off."

"Thanks." I tried.

"Ask your husband," he said. I asked my husband.

It came right out, and he didn't get his hands dirty the way I did.

Never mind. We were already in the car, looking for a map of the city. Of course there was one. Hank had a map. We discussed the route. He was for taking the West Side Highway. I was for going dead-straight. We arrived in five minutes via the West Side Highway. "Good for you," I said.

"Jane Ann used to live up here," he said. His first wife's sister. We had a rueful moment over Jane Ann. She was feisty and mean and a drinker and she lived alone. Once a year Mary went to visit her, at Christmas, and Hank drove her up because, like me, she was afraid of the neighborhood. One Christmas they arrived with a basket of fruit and foil-wrapped cheeses, and a stranger answered the door. "Little Janie?" he said. "She dead. Completely dead. Long time."

He double-parked on a side street. The car in front of us was the color of dog food and had the back window smashed in. We agreed that one of us should wait in the car. I waited with the radio on, the London Fortepiano

Trio playing Mozart. Hank banged the door shut and pulled up his collar against a pelting rain.

I thought of how Hank had looked that morning when he was telling me about being with Alice (I thought of her as Alice and estranged from me, though I had been even closer to her than Hank ever could have been, dammit). I recalled that he flushed as he was talking. Maybe my mother had said the same thing about the tools that Hank had said to me, that they would last longer than the two of them. Or maybe talking was not her power. Maybe her power for Hank was the power of listener. That's what he had said, that she paid attention to him. Right.

Maybe the flush was embarrassment at telling me about being eleven and in love with a pregnant "older woman." Maybe it was exertion from the effort of making up such a big lie.

Now I could also see a different way. It could also have been a signal memory, the kind that wakes the body as well as the mind. It seemed now as if a physical memory of the old days had been talking to him through his blood, and the blush was part of his memory, the memory that he was once the happiest and the strongest and the bravest a boy could be.

She was his mirror, I thought, his mirror that preserved his memory of the old days, of how excellent he was. Her being there with him would have given him the reflection he needed in order to see himself. She would have kept her distance, and that would have been an important part of it. He would never have had enough time with her to become used to himself as she saw him, to take what she provided for him for granted. But he had had enough time with her to feel excellent, and that feeling would have set up a lookout light in him. He wasn't able to get to that light by himself or with anyone else, me, for example, his other women, for other examples.

I wondered what it was that she found in him to reflect back, what it was that I never did find, how it was that she had become related to him in an important way and that I hadn't. Nor he to me.

A lady opened a broken umbrella trimmed in lace next to the car. She was wearing a puffy jacket the size of a comforter. She was bent over and she held the umbrella forward over her head and let the rain run down her back and soak her pillowy coat.

On the way home, Hank wanted to talk about money, wanted everything to be settled so that once we were separated the divorce could go through quickly. I said, Let the lawyers talk. He pulled out an index card on which was written what he would give me every week. I didn't read it. "Thank you," I said. We were on the West Side Highway in a spitting rain alongside the disturbed water in the river. "You're welcome," he said.

There was an awkward moment after we picked up Eliza because neither one of us had planned beforehand what we were going to do when we got home. I decided to go to the grocery store. As I left them, I heard Hank say to Eliza, "What do you do when you've got a big problem?" I missed the first part of her answer. The second was "Go on to something else."

Hank asked if I thought everything would be all right with my lawyer, because, if so, he would move. I said, I think so, "think" because I had sent Hank's changes off only the day before and I hadn't heard from my lawyer. He asked if I had told the Andersons he was moving, because he would be going to the club for lunch today and Henry ate at the club. Yes, I said, I told Claire on the street last month. Hank was wearing a good cotton shirt, white, very white, and his dark pin-striped suit. "You look nice," I said.

He didn't answer, didn't close the door when he left.

It was moving week.

Hallelujah. (I was whispering.)

We were standing in the hall.

There were boxes lined up against the wall.

The boxes were labeled CHINA, JAPAN. I couldn't see what else. The hall was dark.

Hank was packing, saying, "Not going to take much, I have to do this all alone."

"Do you want me to help?"

"No. Not you." Discussion over bowls. He wanted the wooden salad bowl, which had the Christmas wood shavings and acorns and pinecones in it—the scent is supposed to lighten the air. It works. I dumped the shavings on a plate and packed the bowl.

Eliza said, "When are you separating?"

I said, "We've been separated for a while now. It's been happening. It's going to take a long time. Moving boxes is just part of it."

"You mean you're not divorcing?"

"We'll probably divorce, but not for a long time."

Hank was hunched over a box. The tape made a screeching sound as he pulled it out from the roll.

"Separating is going to take a long time," I said again. We were moving toward her room, away from the boxes.

Hank was in the living room now, humming aggressively and dancing to violins. He took long strides and hit the ground hard with his bare feet. Then he was sorting, packing records.

Eliza said, "Is he going to live with the boxes?"

I said, "No, he'll unpack them."

"Not that," she said. "Is he going to live where the boxes are?"

"Well, he travels a lot. He'll live there sometimes."

Hank wanted to discuss lamps. He needed at least two more. He said, Put the ugly one in your bedroom. I put the ugly one in my bedroom. He took the brass one next to his desk, since he already had its mate in the new place.

He went down for the car.

I put Eliza's breakfast on the coffee table in the sitting room. Special treat.

I took the boxes out to the elevator and packed the elevator and rode it down. The doorman said Hank had just gone up when I arrived in the lobby with boxes and a huge photograph of the Watchung Mountains. I stood around for a while, waiting, and then went back up. Hank was in the kitchen, writing instructions to put in potatoes between five-thirty and six.

"What time are you coming home?" I wanted to know.

"I don't know. Maybe six o'clock. I hope you won't be around when the movers come. I don't want you around."

I began rinsing and preparing the chicken so I wouldn't have to do it later. Eliza came into the kitchen and let out a scream.

"What's wrong?" I said, turning my head toward her. My hands were wet with chicken breast.

"You're tearing the chicken apart!"

"I'm just taking the skin off. It's healthier," I said.

"You're ripping it!"

"It's dead," I said. "We're going to eat it for dinner. It will taste good."

"Please stop, please," Eliza said. She was behind me, trying to pin my arms to my sides. I dropped the last chicken breast in the sink.

"It's over, Eliza. I've finished now."

"Your mother likes to rip and tear. Makes her feel powerful," Hank said. He buckled his raincoat and lit his pipe. "Come on, Eliza, walk me to the door."

Two days later he left. It was a Saturday.

Eliza woke early and came to me, saying something she had to repeat a few times because the rain was so loud on the air conditioner. She wanted to know if she could play for a while in her bath. I said yes. She wanted to know if she could watch TV for a while. I said yes. She mouthed, When are you getting out of bed?

"Let's get out of bed," I said. I helped her run a bath. I went into the sitting room. Hank was taking down pictures. He said he would help me move the Sargent poster if I wanted to. I did. Someone had to stand on the rim of the couch to reach high enough to hang it. I said I would. I could see he was afraid. I have good footing in situations like this. He said, "Well, maybe you'll fall down and break your neck." I didn't fall.

He sorted the tools. He told me that I needed to buy new screwdrivers, both kinds, regular and Phillips, and several sizes of each. We moved the record stand to the hall and put an old table in place of the stand, which he was taking. The old table looked great. He said, "Well, you married me for the wrong reasons, but at least you got Eliza." Then he said he didn't want me around while he finished.

I took a jacket and a yellow pad of paper and my pen and some research about currency futures and went down to Jane's. She gave me a cup of green tea and a heating pad and some aspirin. When I went back upstairs I started moving paintings around to cover up some of the bigger blank spaces. The handyman came with his son and another boy and put up my bulletin board.

At first, it didn't seem different. It seemed as if Hank were away on one of his trips, and it wasn't such a big deal that I had the apartment all to myself.

Ordinary things went wrong: A CD jammed in the compact disc player midway between in and out and stuck that way; the dishwasher broke; the geraniums died suddenly; Hank gave Eliza a gerbil and it bit her; I went to the theater a week after the day my ticket was good.

A sad thing happened. Eliza's teacher said she had

started to get up in class, leave the room, walk the halls, and cry. She told the teacher that no one could help her. I asked her what was wrong. She said that Mrs. McDermott had finally said she could bring her gerbil to school, but what was the use if she couldn't handle him and show him around.

At the same time, it was different.

Away from me, Hank acquired a new dimension. My marriage to him seemed remote, but he himself took on a more definite shape. As he became less threatening, he got smaller and also clearer. I had new ideas, questions for him. What chores? I wondered. What did he do for her? Maybe he hosed down the screens, the front porch screens, before he put them up, maybe he fitted the loose bricks back in the dirt in the path to her front door. I could see them standing on either side of this imaginary brick path, admiring the pattern in the bricks, secure in their mutual respect for each other's state of growing. Maybe she was the one who showed him how to arrange his tools, how to take care of them, how to use them properly, maybe she inspired his love for them, and for catalogs, a pursuit I had admired because it was so relentless and rigorous.

What I reasoned was that if Alice had been able to give Hank's emerging life company and protection, enough to make him feel safe and want to learn things, to be in the world, to put his whole body in the world and hold nothing back, which is what he said, I remembered that especially, "hold nothing back," then she must have given me that too. She must have. It was a great bonus to know that I had not gotten all I needed from a place of frog stories and old bedsheets and Kleenex and yellowy feet, that in fact my own mother, my airy sweet young mother, who knew how to do things and was willing to teach, must have loved me too, a little piece of herself all tucked into itself, deeply and impressively loved me. I was almost sorry I had pulled up all the carrots in the fit I had once when Hank complained about my weeding. Almost sorry because by extension it meant her teaching had withered into that inglorious end, that she had taught through Hank something that hadn't been learned.

All in all, I was satisfied and hard to ruffle. On most things.

On the subject of Eliza and me, however, I was as raw as ever. Hank sensed my vulnerability. He played on it, in one note in particular, enclosed with the cleaners' bill: "You're deserting me so you can be alone with her. That way you escape all risk, all surprise, even, or especially, pleasurable surprises. You don't have to worry about what I'm going to say or do. It's what you've always wanted. You'll keep her in a playpen with you, where you can control everything. Pretty soon, she'll want to get out but you won't let her. You'll bombard her with your love, or whatever it is you call it. You'll bury her with it. She'll die with you."

The note was written on one of his new engraved postcards, on which his name and new address stood out, conveying modest hope, like new school supplies. I called him.

"Do you really think I'm using Eliza?"

"What?"

"What you wrote me when you sent me the cleaners' bill."

"I don't remember. Did you pay the bill?" he said.

Eliza and Benjamin grew close again. Benjamin seemed to be leading her out of the magical toward the abstract. Or maybe it was the school. The two of them got deep into atoms and molecules and cells, multiples of life on invisible levels. It was an endless fascination to them that so much of a thing could die and the thing itself remain alive, still be capable of regeneration.

I was involved early on because I was a class mother on the Coventry lower school excursion to the "Inside the Body" exhibit at the science museum. The exhibit reminded me of the Mr. Tooth Decay movies I had seen in grade school. It was thrilling in the same big life-and-death way, only this time it wasn't anybody's fault that things fell apart. There was no lecture on tooth brushing or the consequences of not brushing. This time it was all about life, life coming to be and splitting into new life, and life showing up in the same patterns all up and down the evolutionary scale. It had a visceral twist to it, which I chewed on for a while, the idea that nobody, once a body, can be a fugitive from either life or death.

The children brought home fact-and-activity books that Benjamin and Eliza played with for days. Sometimes they tried out their new ideas on me.

One afternoon, Eliza and Benjamin came into my study to tell me that I looked different.

"I do?"

"I can see your blood cells dying," Eliza said.

"They are popping," said Benjamin.

"I don't feel anything," I said.

"That's the mystery," said Eliza.

"Three million blood cells just popped inside you," said Benjamin.

"I didn't hear anything," I said.

"You just lost a ton of atoms with that breath," Benjamin said to Eliza. He covered her mouth. She pushed him off.

"Stop it," she said.

"You breathed, birdbrain. I'm helping you to stop the killing. You're always breathing."

"So how come I still look the same and feel the same?" I said. I was trying to bring the attention back to me.

"Aha," said Benjamin. "Dum ta dum dum, the mystery."

"How come, Benjamin?" said Eliza.

"I don't know," he said. "I didn't understand that part."

"Do you know, Mom?"

"I think it has to do with a rule about the universe: Nothing in the universe is ever lost but everything is changing all the time into something else."

"Like my mother could be your breath," said Benjamin, I wasn't sure to whom but I answered:

"In a way. I was thinking more like families that come apart and then the people in them move and attach to different people."

"I don't think that's a nice thing to talk about, Mom," Eliza said.

Hank began spending time with a bright Japanese woman from the bank. He introduced Eliza to her. I could not comfort Eliza when she came back with the news. "She's just the right size, not big like you. She fits under his chin."

"Smaller than I am, but bigger than you," I said.

"Yeah," she said, "the right size."

"You know," I said, "hearts are muscles. That makes them elastic. Hearts are very powerful elastic muscles.

They can expand to take in someone new and not lose
what they have."

"She fits under his chin," Eliza repeated.

I let her paint her desk purple. She enjoyed it.

Eliza cultivated her passion for soup, insisting that if I
loved her I would make it for her. She liked vegetable
soup, which took about an hour to eat because she
separated all the vegetables into piles on separate plates
and ate them one vegetable at a time, drinking from the
bowl after all the vegetables were gone.

She developed her own projects. One day she and
Benjamin came home with a new book and a plan. They
shut themselves up in the back of the apartment. They
boiled water. They dyed string. They searched through
Eliza's rock collection for two flat stones. They asked
for things—a small jar, an earthenware pot, jasmine.
There wasn't any jasmine. "You ruined it," she said.

"Ruined what?"

"I knew you would ruin it. You always ruin everything. We were going to do great magic for you and
Dad. But you spoiled it. Come on, Benjamin." They got
their bikes and slammed their way outside.

"Shut the door," I said after them, and went back
into my room. The book was open on the floor. The
rocks held the pages flat down about a third of the way

through the book. "To Cause Love Between Two People," it said. There was a formula: "Take three strings, one each for the colors of the earth, the sun, and the moon . . ."

Later that day I took Eliza and put her on top of a bookcase and gave her a lecture. "There are two things that are true," I said. "The first is that your daddy and I are not ever coming back together again, and the second is that you are not going to marry your daddy."

"So?" she said.

"I just want you to know," I said.

She jumped off the bookcase and went into her room.

Hank and I had one scene in a coffee shop when Hank became excited over the Cropsey landscape. I wanted to sell it and be finished with all the money part of our breakup; he wanted to keep it and look at it. He couldn't afford to be deprived of looking at it, he said, and if I would just sign the painting completely over to him, it would make him feel better, all right, even, and then I would be able to get along with him. Wouldn't I like getting along with him for a change? He said he had nothing to remind him of nature and his boyhood, and he wanted something. He pulled out his handkerchief and said he couldn't even think about it without tears flowing from his eyes. I reminded him that his allergies were such that tears flowed from his eyes when he opened the icebox.

"You don't feel anything, do you, ever?"

"No wonder I didn't feel anything. You were sleeping with my mother."

"We're not talking about that now."

"At least you could have included me."

"I tried to. Anyway, since you bring it up, you're nothing like her, never were, never could be. Not at all like her. You refuse to cook, in fact, you probably can't cook. You don't know how to wear perfume. You don't understand what it is to grow something, to be at home in your garden. There's probably still nothing on your side of the medicine cabinet now."

"My worth is buried in me and speaks for itself. I don't need to add to it."

"What is that supposed to mean?"

"I am long precious metals and short foreign currency."

"Stop it, Kate."

"Fuck off, Hank."

He made an angry swipe at my nose, missed, and knocked his water glass clear off the table. Ice flew in the air and onto his seat. The glass landed in chunks on the floor, tripping a passing waiter. There was a tremendous clatter. Hot coffee and two tuna fish sandwiches, with lettuce, fell onto the floor among the broken dishes. Hank stood up carefully, dripping water and ice and trembling. He was still in the booth. He had to curve like a banana to stay standing. I said, "Can you get out? Try."

"You don't understand anything," he said. "I don't think you can." His voice was very small.

I did understand some things.

I said, "You thought I was a line to her. You thought she must have left her prints on me."

"I had a right to expect that, Kate. Think about it. It was hardly a risk. I had so much genetic info going for me."

Jack Cardiff and I talked in the mornings, after Eliza was off to school, and resumed our lunchtime walks. We walked through wet leaves and dead leaves, sun and fog. I was aware that I often didn't ask Jack how he was, that I was absorbed in my own drama and the way he connected me to it. Hank would have said I was greedy for comfort. I couldn't disagree. I just sat there, holding the phone in my lap on top of the comforter, or walked beside him, at his pace, listening to advice. Practical advice. Soothing advice. Advice about money. Advice about Eliza.

When I was home working, I worked in Eliza's room. I felt most at peace in her room. I liked the way her powder smelled, or maybe it was the soap. Or maybe it was her, herself. It was a way to be with her. It was a safe way to be with her. I wasn't smothering her because she wasn't there, and I couldn't overstay because the phone always rang and took me away. I went from her bed to Jack's voice, from one attachment that made me feel guilty and a dangerous person to another that made me feel incapable of harm and less guilty. It seemed I always had to have something flowing into me, either the smell of her soap all along the bed frame or the vibrations of Jack's voice over the phone.

Jack often said this sentence: "I like you so much." The variations on it were: "I think about you all the time" and "It was hard for me to let you go yesterday."

The effect of his attention was that I began to have tender feelings for him.

I tried to get lost in this tenderness, so strong was my wish to block out all other feelings.

One day I found myself walking on the bridle path, listening to Jack worry that his wives never understood Christmas. I was troubled by how interested I was. I began to worry that I didn't understand Christmas.

The talk about Christmas and wives somehow implicated me, but seemingly not Jack. For me, it was a complicitous act to hear him, but apparently not for him to tell me. He stayed where he was, apart. The world he talked about was "there." But I was mixed up in the world I was hearing about. It was as if my observation, my hearing, though not his telling, might cause one thing, or another, to happen.

I was actually having the same experience with Eliza, but she was quick to stop it. On her school's field day, she directed me to the opposing team, giving me a red-and-yellow signifier to hang around my neck. She stuck a note on it that she watched me read before she whooped away to join her friends. It said: "I am I and you are you. Live it up anyway."

"What does this mean?" I asked her.

"I just made it for you to wear. That's your side," she said, pointing away from her. It turned out that my side was also Benjamin's side, and he was a demon running relays and hopping in sacks and especially cheering on his teammates. He seemed to embrace the whole world, such as it was for him then, bodies planted in burlap. I heard him above everything, urging me on as I stumbled across the green in my sack.

The weekdays began to lose their heaviness. Saturday was still hard. Saturday was a problem for me because Jack didn't call on the weekends, and because Eliza and I were waiting all day for Hank to pick up Eliza and we were both of two minds about it. The two of us were a maze of go/stay, love/hate, play/sulk. It was painful to go through it with her.

One Saturday afternoon, we ran out of errands a few hours too early, so we took the plastic bat and the whiffle ball and went outside. There were some kids in the park, but they were part of a birthday party. Eliza wanted to watch them from the outlying rocks. She sat apart, holding her bat and looking, and I moved about and chatted with the mothers. She was offered a piece of cake, declined, was asked if she wanted to play, said no. I felt desperate as I chatted, sinking on a light, light day. Then some friends came who were unattached. We went over to them. The mom thought up a scavenger hunt. Eliza ran around like crazy, looking for gray rocks, bent sticks, mica. She was happy.

Her father came to find her, announcing he was double-parked. He was angry that she wasn't ready, but he let her finish the hunt while he waited up the hill by the car. I walked her there. "I'll miss you," she said. "I'll see you soon, at five tomorrow," I said. "Stop that," he said. "You'd think she was going away for good." His lips started to disappear but he pushed them out. "Go," he said, "go out on your date." "I'm going to the grocery store," I said, and I walked west into a red sun.

That night I started making room in my house, cleaning out one closet after another, pitching flippers, soccer balls, lingerie catalogs, garden catalogs, photographs, pocketbooks, rocks. Cleaning out reminded me of Isabel Dover. I had a feeling she would approve. Thinking about Isabel reminded me of my own mother, and that reminded me of Hank. I discarded with a vengeance, in the manner of a daisy pull: "He really was her paperboy, he really wasn't; his adoration pleased her, she wouldn't have been able to pick him out from a lineup of two; he really did help her sort and store the bulbs, he learned about bulbs from a book."

For days afterward, I filled the hall with trash. The super was amazed. There was a pleasing brutality about it, a coldness and silence every night by the bloodless heap of trash. I liked looking at it before I went to bed, knowing it would be gone when I woke up.

The Salvation Army visited on a great spring day. They had to make two trips.

Jack and I took a particularly long walk that afternoon through the southern parts of the park, at the end of which he told me that many men, men nowadays, don't want to sleep with women because that means proving themselves. They find all sorts of excuses not to do it: "Women live in an ocean of feelings and sex, and men say that's a compartment off to the side; why is she making so much trouble?"

"What do they want to do?" I asked.

"They want to go out to dinner," he said.

We were coming down the hill and just about to emerge from the park. It was dusk and we were not in a safe part. He said something that I can't quite remember. It might have been "I worry about you."

We were standing on the sidewalk on the park side, waiting for a cab and talking. He was in back of me with his hands on my shoulders, lightly rocking me back, toward him, and then forth, when he held on tighter to my shoulders. A taxi pulled up. With uncharacteristic speed, he presented himself in front of me. He reached for the door and I moved forward to get in. He pulled the door back, moving away from me. It was a stiff gesture, as if the door were a cape and he were performing a ritual move with it. I saw him look across the street, and plant his mind there, as far away as his eyes could go, as if he were taking himself away from what he was doing, helping a woman he had just taken a two-hour walk in the park with into a taxicab because it was time, and besides, they had come too close to his own neighborhood.

I looked back at him from inside the cab, where I was still crouched from bending myself over to get in. He glanced down at me and nodded his head and with the same stiffness, in the manner of a performance, resumed his stare across the street. I heard the door slam and I saw him put his hands in the pockets of his coat and turn away. He was going forward, but the taxi wasn't moving yet. His head was erect and lined up with his body.

I fix these images because it was exactly at the point at which I saw him stare across the street, away from me, that I felt a violent jolt. I saw him staring at where he would soon go, back to his marriage, and his apartment that was flooded with light no matter what time of day. I felt his leaving of me, his body retreating as he pulled the door open for me, and I felt me getting inside the taxi as if I were entering a box, a small, dark box, and then felt him again, moving toward a place built in the light to exist in the light. My will was to rail against being left in the dark box and to insist on an attachment to him that I knew was hopeless and moreover did not want. Yet I could not shut down the wish for it that within seconds had gutted my insides, when I saw the look he gave to the street when he didn't want to look at me. The moment I sensed his turning away, my interest in him came alive and flowered into an aggressive despair.

"This is not it. Keep going." I heard that voice inside me, to which another voice, also inside, replied, "You feel something now, don't you? What else do you want?"

Jack and I have come through the zoo to a tree in a clearing in the park, near Fifth Avenue. He turns to look up the hill and we head for a tree with big, low branches. It is a good climbing tree. We lean against it. He says he has conversations in his head with me about whether I desire him or not, and that sometimes I do and sometimes I don't, and the worst is if I think of him as a parent.

And I tell him yes, I care for him, no, I don't think he's my father, because my lawyer is my father now, yes, I would like to sleep with him, yes, I would like to talk to him about his feelings for me and my feelings about him but I don't talk to him about feelings because he is married and I am not.

I thought his question was the general one: Am I desirable in general? was what he wanted to know. And I had told him yes, and with my telling freed him to go on and find someone who was less encumbered by scruples than I was. As I kept talking, I myself began to feel worse and worse, and I could feel him beginning to feel better and better. He was reassured.

He moved away from me slightly as we leaned on our tree. He looked out toward the top of the hill. I was facing the other way, and from time to time I turned to look at him looking up the hill, feeling free. But I didn't feel free because, partly because, I had lied.

His hand was positioned in such a way that I could see it was ten to six and I said, "You have to go now, it's ten to six." He looked irritated and finished what he was saying about how he hadn't maybe been as honest as he might have been, about how he sometimes envied my lightness about family, about how he had been too heavy and maybe I had been too light, and also that he tried not to talk about how he felt about me in a way that would manipulate me. There was a heavy, watery sensation inside me. We walked down the hill. The grass is thick there; it's wild things, but it had been mowed recently and smelled of summer. The grass under my feet came up to meet me.

"Do you think that sex is a substitute for everything else or that everything else is a substitute for sex?" I asked him.

"Sex is what's real," he said. He seemed very sure about his answer.

The following day Eliza was to go off with her father to Whitby Cove. A clinking sound woke me. Eliza was next to me, emptying her monkey bank. She wanted me to get dressed because she had things to do.

"I'm getting up," I said, not budging.

"Hurry," she said. I hurried.

We went out on her errands. She bought three lottery tickets for her father. "He really needs to win," she said. We shopped for new sneakers and she left at noon with her father for vacation in the country.

That afternoon, Jack and I stayed outside until dusk,

walking the park while he told me once again the story of his first marriage without leaving out one detail. Then abruptly:

"I am talking too much."

"No" (a lie).

"I am boring you."

"No" (another lie), at which point . . .

Her arms go around his neck.

His neck falls forward toward her.

Lips meet.

Meet again.

Heads rest in the curve of other's neck.

A rat runs across a fallen tree branch.

Only she sees.

The wide world, she thinks. The woods. The park. The great world.

Softball players in red shirts with white script go past, two at a time, one at a time, sometimes three.

And beyond the pair of us are the buildings, the skyline, a white, faint moon. Shadow.

"Before we're too old, Kate," he said. "Because women, you know, always say something. 'It's the wind,' they say."

First it's a wave. Then it's particles.

And so he comes in and I am happy to see him, and his lips are moving in a nonthreatening way and he follows me into the kitchen and I say, Are you hungry? and he answers, Yes, and I pick up the kettle and turn and he catches me with the empty kettle and puts his arms around me and I have mine around his neck, still holding the empty kettle, and he is kissing me, still very soft, and I sigh, and he stops. I put some water in the kettle and put it on the stove and turn up the flame. He is behind me, putting his arms around my waist. It feels good and I am glad I have already gone out and done my errands. He has his hands under my shirt and with one he unhooks my bra and with the other unzips my jeans, which don't fall. He picks me up in his arms and bends down so I can turn off the flame, and he carries me, not too easily, though he is strong, to the bed.

All hell breaks loose, so to speak. We do not say a word.

He leaves at six o'clock and comes back at one the next day. We play out an almost identical scene. Except it's a little shorter. And the next day a little shorter. And so on. It seems necessary to shrink the action so as not to lose the intensity, which nevertheless diminishes. The light, too. It begins to seem like no light at all, casting no shadow but instead bringing out a dinginess day by day that at first was not apparent, in the curtains, in the lamps, in the painted bureau, in me. As the light decays, it brings forth decay.

There are bright moments without fold or shadow. I

remember coming in on a day that was too hot, coming into the kitchen from the bath. I was pulling my dress over my head, and he was sitting in the rocking chair waiting for me. I hadn't known he was already in the house. I didn't think anyone was in the kitchen, and there he was, waiting for me, watching me pull my dress over my head.

There are warnings: "Darling, this is for you, Darling." Who was this Darling and what was he offering her when he summoned her when he burst inside her, and at no other time, "Darling."

There is a dire warning: When I did not recognize his voice on the telephone.

After the first week, I carried wishes in my head. The wish to be aware when it was the last time but constantly having to throw away the last time because there was one more time. The wish to confuse our bodies, a wish that comes true, though not happily: Soon I could not tell if the noise was coming from his mouth into my ears or my ears into his mouth: "Darling." And I could not stop the word, "Darling."

At first the walls of my bedroom recede from us when we are there, an abrupt and tremendous expansion of space, as if, on entering, we broke through the wall of the world, sprawling into solid light. Then my room becomes a place of mystery, of familiar mystery, not at all the kind of place where the world opens but the kind of place you find yourself, a darkening place, in fact dark everywhere except for one place, an opening of light that he goes through at his pleasure. I form the idea that by attaching myself to him I will somehow attach myself to the way out. An old, familiar thing happens. He gets up and leaves and I don't.

The proportions of the day change. There is more time spent ironing the sheets at night and more time choosing the fruit at the market in the morning than there is time spent in the room, which seems itself to become smaller with the passing of the days and the repetition of our play together. And it's clear that all that washing and arranging and ironing and lettuce and tomato sandwiches and meeting in the bed will soon come to an end.

So that by the time Eliza returns from three weeks with her father, there is no question anymore of where Jack will meet me now that we can no longer carry on in a small room in the back of my house.

It must have rained all that next September, rain and fog and mist and drip. Nights and days so like one another, dark, damp, sticky days, only slightly darker, damp, sticky nights, every creature, it seemed, waiting for a break, for cool air. It was a season of monoclimatic experience once again and it was intense. It was in that dangerous period where survival depends on abiding by the cardinal rules of trading: Cut your losses and get yourself to believe that an essential ingredient of winning is that it's okay to lose.

Nothing was okay at the moment, as far as I was concerned. I felt as if I had fallen into a period of neglect, which couldn't have been true since there was no one to neglect me. But I took everything personally. I even took it personally when the cat started avoiding me and was hardly seen during the day. I embarked on a campaign to lure her out from Eliza's room with the cat-bouncing wire toy. That was a success. Cranny loved her toy so much that she would follow it, with me holding the other end, out into the street and across into the park, where I worked in the clubhouse in the rain on their computer system, setting up tennis ladders and appointment calendars for the coaches. There wasn't much business at the courts, so I didn't have too much to do there, but I did install a new way to track the inventory. And, weather permitting, I watched the tennis.

Cranny and I took some melancholy turns around the reservoir. She was a lot faster than Jack but she didn't have a voice and I missed Jack's voice. We met him one afternoon and I told him that.

"I miss your voice and your body and everything about you," he said.

"Sounds like a lot," I said. The truth was, everything about me missed him terribly, but I also knew I would have missed anybody terribly.

"I guess this is as good a place as any to have this conversation," he said. And he began to talk about getting on the train and off the train. He remembered I had said I was not looking forward to another fall and winter, and he said, "But I was going one direction and you were going the other, and you were getting unmarried and I didn't get on the train."

I had no trouble following this, having heard about this train a lot before.

"I sometimes wonder if anything happened," I said.

He said, "It happened. I fell in love. I hadn't expected it and I did. It has never happened to me before, well, not since I was twenty, anyway." Then he said, "On that note," and squeezed my arm and turned to face a group who were coming off the far court. He raised his tennis racquet in a salute and went forward to greet them.

I watched him, taking for myself a good long look at his legs.

That same day I became single-minded about the floor. I researched until I found Tomas, a Hungarian, whose life was all about floors. I left a message on his machine. Two days later he called: "You message me about your floor. What can I to do?" He came the next day. He apologized for his English: "Sorry just in Hungary language—here born, here was the school. This dilemma my. I want to die United States. I definitely have to meet everyday with that people who live here. Difficult. Difficult." I started to cry. It was terribly awkward, but he quickly redirected my attention: "Water on wood, madame, not good."

Together we got on hands and knees and inspected the dining-room floor. He made a noise with his tongue. "I am sorry," he said. "I love floor. Much exciting the floor and I trusting myself. I definitely interested in your floor, madame, but look, I am sorry. I show you." He ran his hand over the grain in the wood he had just exposed. "My hundred-percent respect is for your floor. But this too long covered. From this will never be color. Only darker the wood growing." I asked him if he would consider taking up the tiles and then we would look at the whole dark floor and make a decision about what to do with it. He pecked at it and thought. He said, "What you give me I give you back. At fifteen in Hungary, was must hold the machine." He stood up and rattled his body as if he had hold of a machine too powerful for him. "Was must sanding the floor and not scratch. At fifteen, madame. Don't laugh for me." (I wasn't.) He went on: "Maybe this is just bug in my head. I know so many things that others know not.

Everybody specializing himself, I for floors. Would be good to show to someone."

He massaged the floor and thought some more and said that the floor would be perfect after he was finished with it. Then he would come and photograph it. He showed me how good it would make him feel. "Much satisfaction in my work. When I take picture of my work and I see it, I almost fly." We made a date to remove the tiles and work on the floor.

When he came back, Tomas hung plastic sheets that covered the walls and the entrances to the dining room and the sitting room and blocked off the living room.

There was machine noise for two days, then sounds of hand work. On the third evening, Tomas removed the shrouds and invited Eliza and me into the dining room. He told Eliza about the wood not having space to breathe and how not having space to breathe had killed it, almost killed it, but that he had been able to rescue it. We all got on our hands and knees. "It looks perfect," I said. "Of course," he said. He continued to wipe the floor with a scrub brush dipped in a coating. Eliza wanted to try, and Tomas made a place for her and gave her a paintbrush, and for a short while we were together again in our source of satisfaction.

I would like to be able to tell you that this story ended very neatly, with all our situations resolved, that something like this happened: Hank's girlfriend turned out to be a crackerjack baseball player, like Benjamin's mother, and that she became the coach for Benjamin's park team and that made her okay in Eliza's eyes, or at least someone she didn't have to be preoccupied with. And Hank and I rooted like bandits from the stands every week, growing more familiar than we had ever been, so that little by little the defensive walls we had put up in our marriage fell away and in their place grew what Augustine called the bright boundary of friendship. I would like to be able to tell you that I found my calling on the courts and that Eliza did too, and that's where all our mother/daughter struggling and reconciliation took place and where we both became champions in our own right, always giving it our all, playing our hearts out and winning many tournaments.

But in fact it was just the normal hodgepodge of disintegration and partial regeneration and always a little lost and longing left in the tissues.

Some things began to drift into a past where they change from objects of nonregret to regret. Eliza's father became part of that part of my past. A fondness for him set in, like a break in the weather. I missed him standing in the kitchen, drinking the orange juice out of the carton. It became easier to be with him, though I never did figure out whether he really knew Alice or not. Little

tests I devised for him he passed. He could fold a newspaper like a paperboy quicker than I could do a hospital
corner. He had a loose-limbed natural newspaper
throw. He was accurate. It amused him that I gave him
these tests, which I administered while he was waiting
for Eliza to get ready to go with him on their weekends.

On the other hand, I didn't want Hank to have
known my mother, and it was too neat anyway if he
had, like a magazine story, and so I stonily refused to
acknowledge it, to him.

It was on the court after the pro had just boinked the
daylights out of me that Hank and I came the closest we
ever came to a clarifying conversation.

Hank had never seen me play tennis before and he
was impressed. I wasn't embarrassed to have lost because I had played so well. Besides I had my remarkable
cat with me. I picked her up from the towel she was
sleeping on and draped her around my shoulders and
walked tall over to the fence.

His first words were:

"I see you've trained the cat."

"I think it's my talent."

"Do you take her with you all the time?"

"Just about."

"I don't think your mother played tennis."

"My aunt."

"Your aunt, of course, your aunt. Why did you stop?"

"It's a game."

"So?"

"I got very good at losing. I thought it would carry over and mess up my mind. It's what my aunt said. I think she was right."

"So what are you going to do?"

"I'm not sure yet. I would like to learn how to repair things."

"What things?"

"Surface things."

"Surface things like?"

"A marriage."

"Don't mock me, Kate."

"Just kidding. Computers, maybe."

"That's not surface."

"I know, I said I was just kidding."

"You confuse me."

"Good."

"Good?"

"I don't know. I'm sorry. I'm just sorry."

We were looking at each other through the mesh. We had the cat between us too. I held the cat and he reached through the mesh to work the muscles around her ears.

"Okay," I said. "Now I want to listen. I will hear you if you tell me. I'm ready."

"About Alice?"

"I want to listen to you tell me about Alice. I wasn't ready before. And I only want to know what is true, just what is true."

"How much difference will it make?"

"Look, are you going to tell me anything or not because if you aren't . . ."

"Would you bring Cranny to my side? I haven't seen her for a while."

I left the court and went to him. We talked for an hour or more in the fresh air, the cat calm in his lap. With our words splayed out amid clumps of grass, dandelion puffs, deadwood, dogwood, insects, and small animals, we covered a great deal of ground.

A lot of it was new, and it unsettled me to hear it.

Part of it was about estimating, but it was mostly a story of lilacs and gardens and black snakes and birds' nests, a story of pulling down honeysuckle, tracing poison ivy vines back to their roots, sawing out old deadwood, removing some of the older trunks, of how, when they had finished a good afternoon's work, they would sit together in the screened-in porch. Toward the end of summer her feet began to swell, and he would take her feet into his own hands and rub them and they would talk. She taught him to identify the wild cherry trees, the leaves of which fed tent caterpillars and red-spotted purple butterflies, the long grasses where the pheasants retreated to do their mating dance in private, winter-berry, inkberry. She told him her dream of planting species of grasses in the clay soil, native grasses like little bluestem and prairie dropseed.

I would have been completely blown away with his romantic talk and erotic intimations about my mother's feet, the like of which I had never heard from him before, had it not been for the fact that I had inadvertently read something quite similar the previous morning when I turned to the wrong section of the paper for a continuation of a basketball game account and picked up on a yesteryear's-lifestyle column. Let it be, I thought to myself.

Instead, I said, "You should stop reading whatever books you are reading."

"What books?" he said.

"Yesterday's newspapers, then," I said.

"Touché," he said. Then, "You'll just never know, will you?"

"I could find out," I said.

"I know. But you won't."

"You're probably right." Then, "Anyone could have taught you estimating."

"Can't fool you, can I, babychuck."

He put his head in my lap then and I thought I felt something pass between us, an interrupted and incomplete connection between a man and a woman, or maybe between the seen and the unseen. I imagined this, but I did not dismiss the idea of it. Without tenderness, we are in hell. And with it? With it, things are better.

"Alice," he said, into my thighs.

"I'm Kate, Hank," I said.

"Be Alice again," he said. "Just for a minute."

And then Cranny climbed up his side, over his ribs and nestled down, as far as a cat can nestle down into a crew cut.

Epilogue

After that, not too long afterward, there was a general lightening in the tone of the days, which were now punctuated with unportentous detail: Cranny's paw-shakes. Benjamin's jokes (Question: Why doesn't anyone ever want to eat with basketball players? Answer: Because they always dribble). Eliza's fortune-telling (for Benjamin: A yellow leaf will fall on your head; for me: You will go north).

Work picked up at the bank, the result of a merger. I was assigned to meld some of the protocols of the new subsidiary into the company personnel booklet. At the same time, I began to teach tennis to little ones on Saturday. In return, the tennis pro played with me and

I improved. It wasn't enough of a life yet to dam the past and leave it where it happened. I still had a feeling of being flooded.

One thing did become clear in regard to Eliza and me. It became clear that it wasn't me who had to do anything. Eliza would do it herself. Out of self-defense, she would lock me out. It was just as Isabel had said. Eliza taught me how to let her go. She taught me how to let her leave and how she would stay at the same time. It seemed effortless, as if an instinct, a life instinct, asserted itself within her. It wasn't pleasant. But it was effective.

When I complained about the turtlenecks on the bathroom floor or the homework smashed up in the book bag or the peanut-butter splots on the counter, she'd give me a look of tolerance.

She asked, hopefully, when I was going to start to go to an office every day and come home late like all the other mothers. She learned to scowl and practiced, particularly, I thought, around me. I remarked that I thought she should accord her dad and me equal treatment, equal good moods. She put down her book to deliver: "Isn't it enough that I'm more comfortable with you?"

She insisted on a quotient of nostalgia, keeping the photo boxes on the bottom shelves of the bookcases for easy access, though she rarely looked at them. She wanted the costume wardrobe moved into her bedroom, which we did, though it made the bedroom crowded and hard to clean up. She developed a game of laying all the pieces of every costume on all the surfaces of her room, hardly ever making up new ones but sticking to what I told her had been part of the original ensembles. Unless a costume had a history that involved her original family, it wasn't worth anything to her.

One evening I was picking up the room, reminding her to set out her clothes for the next day and find her homework and not forget to put the witch hat back in the wardrobe, when she asked me to tell her about the time when she and I and her dad wore the baboon costumes. When Eliza was two months old we had all dressed up as "the First Family" and gone to a fund-raising party at the Museum of Natural History. "Later," I said. "We're busy."

"I'm trying to have a quiet time with you about the old days and you keep telling me to do things. I'm sad now."

"Thinking about the old days makes you sad?"

"Yes."

"I can understand that. Don't you want to stop now?"

"No. I want you to help me find my mask."

"You didn't have a mask. You were too little. You just had the suit. I made it from one of your coveralls."

"I know where that is," she said, and she dove in and came up with a tiny black-and-brown thing and two big baboon masks. "I think I'll hang these up," she said, and she took down one of her drawings from the bulletin board and in its place pinned the masks, side by side, with her baboon coveralls underneath them. They are still there.

They are still there, and they remind me that it's only recently that I myself can tolerate the idea that what is lost cannot be found, despite however many recovery attempts by however obstinate a person. It can't be found because it's on the other side of words. It came before thought and was lost before words.

Language is born of that loss. It's one way we try to get back, to recoup the distance between what was and what is, to say what it was that was lost, and is repeatedly lost day after day. Language says to the separate one: "Would you stand back, honey, because I want to get a better look." First, of course, you have to agree to be separate, and this is a sticky point. Then, too, there is a difference between the absence of connection and the experience of every connection as an absence. Part of the story could lie in that difference, although, let's face it, it could lie in anything. Everything is part of the story. Every gesture is a search for something we have all lost.

There was the time, for example, I brought home a skirt, one of those casual, loose skirts that you can wear any day, anywhere. Eliza saw it and, quite uncharacteristically, put it on. It fit her in a completely different way but it suited her much better than it suited me. It surprised us both, and it also surprised us how very glad we were about such a simple thing, a simple ordinary thing like how supple things can be—including us, Eliza and I, and the cloth of the skirt and the curves of the trees as they blew in the wind outside the window that framed Eliza, who was swaying in front of me, her hands directing the flow of the skirt as it moved and her head held so high and with such proprietary assurance. I myself felt light, much, much lighter, and also fully clothed.

I did not lose the conviction that there will always be one more thing to say, or a better way to say it, that there is no such thing as a last word.

It's just that there are many last words and things that show you what the last words were, in case you didn't hear them. So many things come and pass like breath; memory continuously bleeds into the present: Hank swallowing air under arching trees, holding himself against a gravestone, not a muscle moving in his large body, light coming out of the earth, Hank as still as if caught on something, Hank with his hefty tools, or by himself on the hard wet sand of the riverbank, listening.

Memory widens our world, making more of a person than he can hold on to.

We are so often swamped by our cockeyed longings, all of us looking for the faraway one inside the near one, Hank looking in me for my mother, me looking in Eliza for an earlier Eliza or an earlier me, Eliza still holding the secret of where she would look and for whom, everybody trapped in misalliance, keeping busy anyway, patiently untying the knots, patiently tying new knots, lest we be brought to a standstill by that unsolvable knot, that nothing is final and everything is final, that we are at all times attached to the world and that at all times we cannot grasp it. Or if by chance we grasp it, it is only to find that we ourselves have changed and that the world we have is not the one we want now.

That we will always miss our mark or that our mark will miss us is the great joke and the great game of time.

From time to time I remember my arm on Isabel's shoulder, my fingers on her bones. I have come to accept these moments as tokens of some real thing, the real thing, our job being to sort out what belongs to what, what doesn't belong at all. In separation begins the individual.

I get a lot of help from Eliza.

So?

So Eliza and I are outside, waiting for the bus for

school. It is at least six minutes late. I am reading a story in the paper about a man who got so involved in his work as a pastry cook that he got stuck in his kneading machine and had to be taken, along with the machine, to the hospital for surgical separation. "There's a lesson," I say to myself.

Eliza is twirling around the canopy pole. "Stop scraping your shoe on the sidewalk," I say.

"I wish the bus would come now," she says.

"Maybe it will," I say.

"Now is over," she says, and takes another turn around the pole.

About the Author

SUSAN CHACE is a former *Wall Street Journal* reporter and the author of the novel *Intimacy*. This is her second novel.

About the Type

This book was set in Sabon, a typeface designed by the well-known German typographer Jan Tschichold (1902–74). Sabon's design is based on the original letterforms of Claude Garamond and was created specifically to be used for three sources: foundry type for hand composition, Linotype, and Monotype. Tschichold named his typeface for the famous Frankfurt typefounder Jacques Sabon, who died in 1580.